"I'm sorry know you?"

Who on earth was he? Hilary had never seen him before.

He smiled, and two amazing dimples flashed. "We've never met, but we definitely know *of* each other. I'm Conner St. George."

Conner St. George! Oh, she knew of him all right. He was the original Mr. Trouble.

When she didn't answer he repeated, "St. George? Your cousin Marlene was married to my brother Tommy?"

"Of course," she said, nodding her head. "Marlene has spoken of you often in her letters."

"Good things, I hope."

The comment was casual—he didn't even expect an answer. But it was so far from the truth that a slow burn traveled up Hilary's neck. Yes, she'd heard a lot about him. But there had been nothing good....

KATHLEEN O'BRIEN, who lives in Florida, started out as a newspaper feature writer, but after marriage and motherhood, she traded that in to work on a novel. Kathleen likes strong heroes who overcome adversity, which is probably the result of her reading all those classic novels featuring tragic heroes when she was younger. However, being a true romantic, she prefers *her* stories to end happily!

Books by Kathleen O'Brien

HARLEQUIN PRESENTS
1011—SUNSWEPT SUMMER
1189—WHITE MIDNIGHT
1267—DREAMS ON FIRE
1355—BARGAIN WITH THE WIND
1515—BETWEEN MIST AND MIDNIGHT

Don't miss any of our special offers. Write to us at the following address for information on our newest releases.

Harlequin Reader Service
P.O. Box 1397, Buffalo, NY 14240
Canadian address: P.O. Box 603,
Fort Erie, Ont. L2A 5X3

KATHLEEN O'BRIEN

When Dragons Dream

Harlequin Books

TORONTO • NEW YORK • LONDON
AMSTERDAM • PARIS • SYDNEY • HAMBURG
STOCKHOLM • ATHENS • TOKYO • MILAN
MADRID • WARSAW • BUDAPEST • AUCKLAND

For Michaela—
my sister, friend and mother-pretend—
with love and thanks

ISBN 0-373-11600-4

WHEN DRAGONS DREAM

Copyright © 1993 by Kathleen O'Brien.

CHAPTER ONE

MEN!

Hilary Fairfax, sitting in the crowded courthouse hall next to her weeping sister, gritted her teeth until her temples ached. *It's always a man, isn't it?*

She wrapped her arm around Terri's shoulder, trying to quell the soft trembling and labored breathing. Pretty soon they'd call Terri into the hearing room, and she wouldn't want *that man* to see her like this.

But the shaking continued. *Damn the man!* Hilary had hoped, prayed, that Terri's crying was finished forever, but now here she was, dragged into a divorce hearing, stirring up the miserable muck once again. And all for the love of a creep who wasn't good enough to clean Terri's shoes.

"It's okay, honey." Hilary squeezed Terri's shoulder bracingly. "His wife's lawyer just wants to know basic stuff about his money, his condo, presents, stuff like that. Nobody's going to give you a morals lecture. They know you thought he was divorced. They only care about the money."

But Terri didn't answer. She stared at her hands, which she wrung ceaselessly in her lap, and gulped for air.

The hard, angry spot inside Hilary grew harder and angrier. This was so wrong. Terri was only nineteen years old. She was leaving for college tomorrow. She should be packing, laughing, planning, anything but sobbing on this bench, wedged in next to a foul-smelling derelict waiting to get into the courtroom for God knew what.

As furious tears pricked at her own eyes, Hilary blinked quickly. She had to get hold of herself. It wouldn't help either of them if she started bawling. Taking a deep breath, she sat up straighter and for distraction scanned the motley crowd milling in the corridor.

Surprising how many people were still around late on a Friday afternoon. Was everyone here, as Terri was, to give evidence in some tawdry legal squabble? The glossy brown hearing-room doors, all anonymously alike and all tightly shut, gave no clues.

The people were easier to read. The lawyers, for example, were a breeze to spot. Well-dressed, serene, even smug, compared to the anxious-looking witnesses. And Terri wasn't the only person crying. Just in front of them was another young woman, who stood with her back against the wall, her arms folded tightly across her chest, tears falling unchecked down pale cheeks. Probably man trouble, too. Hilary sighed, a deep sound of disgusted resignation. An errant son, a hopeless husband, a disloyal boyfriend. But a man, she'd be willing to bet. Whenever you saw a woman breaking her heart, it was always over a man.

Her glance moved on, then stopped. A man. A man like him, maybe. The one who stood two benches away, talking to what had to be a lawyer. Now *that* was the kind of man she despised on sight—a little like her philandering father, a little like the egotistic president of her senior class in high school, a little like a movie star. Bank on it—he was somebody's trouble, with a capital *T*.

She studied him, indulging her admittedly narrow-minded prejudices with the same bitter pleasure she might feel pressing hard on a sore tooth. What exactly didn't she like? *Oh, let me count the ways*.

Well, she didn't like the way the blue-gray of his expensive suit had obviously been chosen to match his eyes. She didn't like his eyes, for that matter. Men with eyes like that, all drop-dead sensuality under arrogantly arched brows, were too accustomed to getting their own way. And that square jaw. It was a stubborn fighter's jaw. It didn't belong with those eyes, or with those damn dimples that dug into his cheeks every time he smiled down at his lawyer friend.

And something in the way he held himself positively screamed masculinity. He probably ate boiled broken hearts for breakfast. "Theresa Fairfax?" The hearing-room door swung open, and a man peered out at them. Terri looked up with a jerk.

"Take a deep breath, honey," Hilary whispered, nudging her sister to her wobbly feet. "And hold your head high. You didn't do anything wrong. It's not your fault he's a lying creep."

Terri's answering smile was uncertain, but Hilary was pleased to see her chin rise, just a little.

"Over here," Hilary called to the man at the door, who had begun to look dubiously up and down the hall. Terri straightened her belt, threw one last miserable glance over her shoulder at Hilary and disappeared into the hearing room.

Hilary had to grip the hard wooden seat of the bench to keep from following her. Her baby sister, alone in that room with the lawyers and the creep. Her legs tensed, some cave-woman instinct for vengeance coiling her muscles to spring and fight.

But she held herself down somehow, consoling herself with the thought that the creep's wife would probably pummel him quite satisfactorily, legally if not physically.

That would have to suffice. Shutting her eyes, Hilary took the deep breath she'd advised for Terri. *Men!*

"Hello, Miss Fairfax." Suddenly, as though her expostulation had summoned him, a deep masculine voice spoke above her. The surprise turned her deep breath into a choke. "May I sit down?" Her eyes flew open. Who on earth...? Her mouth opened in a soundless "Oh" of disbelief. It was the man she had been watching only moments ago. Mr. Trouble.

He gestured to the empty seat beside her. "May I?"

She didn't answer at first, her mind locked in a slow, stunned search for logic, like an overtaxed computer scanning for a file. Searching, but finding none. How did he know her name? She didn't know him, that much was certain.

Had he perhaps heard the summons for Terri and put the names together? Maybe, but even so, what did he want? Had he singled her out for flirtation, some light banter to pass the time? Doubtful. Hilary had no false modesty; she knew that, with her long auburn hair, large green eyes and slim figure, she was a passably pretty twenty-six-year-old woman. But she wasn't *this* man's type. She had none of the glamour-kitten, come-hither sexiness her intuition told her he preferred.

But even if his request made no sense, she still had no reason to refuse him the seat.

"All right," she said numbly, though every instinct told her it was a bad idea. Up close he seemed more dangerous than ever. His dark brown hair was very thick, with a strong wave just above his forehead. On each side of his wide brow a flash of silver cut through the brown, like captured lightning. And those eyes really were just too much. If he noticed her reluctance, though, he ignored it. He gave a meaningful but wordless glance to the derelict, who with only an inarticulate grumble shuffled over to the next bench.

"Your secretary told me where I could find you," he said, settling in, his elbow on the armrest so that his body was angled toward her. "I waited until your sister was called. She looked like she needed you more than I did."

More than *he* did? Hilary's frown deepened as her bewilderment increased. It was like a bad dream in which you're shoved onstage in the middle of the first act but you've never seen the script.

"I'm sorry," she said slowly, trying to strike the right balance, not too rude, not too forthcoming. He didn't *look* like a nut, but... "Do my sister and I know you?"

He smiled, and the amazing dimples flashed, as if on cue. "We've never actually met, but we definitely know *of* each other." He held out a hand. "I'm Conner St. George."

Conner St. George! Instinct must have pushed her own hand forward, because her brain was in no condition to send coherent signals. Conner St. George. Oh, God, she knew of him, all right. Enough to know that her earlier assessment had hit a bull's-eye. Conner St. George was the original Mr. Trouble.

"St. George?" he was repeating, a slight query in his voice. She must look unbelievably bovine—her mouth hanging open, her eyes staring, as though she didn't recognize the name. "Your cousin Marlene was married to my brother Tommy?"

"Of course," she said, nodding her head and dragging her jaw shut. "Marlene has spoken of you often in her letters."

"Good things, I hope."

The comment was a casual one—perfunctory, really. He didn't even expect an answer. But it was so far from the truth that a slow, hideous burn traveled up Hilary's neck and over her cheeks. Good things? Hardly. Marlene hated Conner St. George. "And he hates me," Marlene had written in her last letter. "He hates me because I loved Tommy, which is more than *he* ever did."

In the three months since Tommy St. George had died in a boating accident, Marlene had written of little else. Conner, the brother-in-law who had not wanted her to marry Tommy. Conner, the stingy tyrant who controlled Tommy's money. Conner, who was too wrapped up in his business to pay any attention to her.

Yes, Hilary had heard a lot about him. But there had been nothing good.

Hilary's face still burned, and she could imagine how she looked right then. Redheads should never get angry or embarrassed—it showed too clearly on their transparent complexions. *Clown cheeks,* an old despised nickname, echoed in a childish singsong in her mind, and the top of her scalp prickled with uncomfortable awareness.

As the silence lengthened, Conner's gaze roamed across her flaming cheeks, and she thought she saw a flicker of sardonic humor in the blue-gray depths of his eyes.

"I see. Well, that's too bad," he said softly. "She speaks more flatteringly of you."

So he was well aware of what Marlene thought of him! And, judging by that small smile, the knowledge merely amused him, as an unloving adult might be amused by the helpless tantrums of a provoking child.

Hilary's anger, set smoldering by Marlene's reports over these past three months, ignited. Damn him, Marlene wasn't a child. She was a heartbroken nineteen-year-old widow. His own brother's widow. And she was pregnant. Pregnant with his brother's child.

And still he dared to be unkind to her. Hilary, who loved Marlene deeply, in spite of her faults, bristled. Narrowing her green eyes, she straightened her back. Why, for civility's sake, should she pretend that either she or Marlene liked him? He didn't bother with civility. He was a selfish bastard and he was making Marlene's life thoroughly miserable.

"Marlene is very dear to me," she said coolly, glad to feel the blood receding from her cheeks. "She's like another sister to Terri and me."

"Good," he said, continuing to smile. "I'm pleased to know she wasn't exaggerating the relationship."

Hilary found his tone offensive, suggesting that Marlene was prone to dramatic exaggerations. And though she had to admit Marlene could be a bit theatrical, hearing him say it annoyed her.

"She *couldn't* exaggerate the relationship," she corrected firmly. "We're family."

"Good," he repeated, apparently unfazed by the subtle reprimand. "Because Marlene needs someone right now. You do know she's pregnant?"

Hilary nodded impatiently. Of course she knew.

"Okay. Well, she's staying at my mountain house until the baby's born." His voice didn't change, but Hilary thought she detected a subtle note of displeasure. And, as she tried to envision this perfectly tailored, coolly competent man living with the haphazard, volatile Marlene, she could understand why.

"Lately, Marlene seems very depressed. I'm not sure why. Perhaps she's lonely. I'm involved in a business deal that's taking up quite a bit of my time, so she often has only my housekeeper for company. She needs someone, and you and your sister are all she's got in the way of family."

"Oh, really?" Grappling with her rising fury, Hilary met his eyes with a hard gaze. Every syllable he uttered was devoid of any normal sympathy for a woman in Marlene's position. Alone in a mountain cottage, alone with her quite natural fears of pregnancy and motherhood? Alone with memories of her young husband, who had drowned only three months before? Well, who wouldn't be depressed?

So what if Conner hadn't wanted his brother to marry Marlene? That didn't exempt him from showing common decency, did it? And that sentence about Marlene having no family! God, the man was insufferable!

"She has you, hasn't she?" Hilary let the ice be heard in her voice. "After all, you *are* her brother-in-law."

He waved away her comment. "I won't be there much until the Dragon's Creek deal is finished," he said, then seemed to realize, with some surprise, that Hilary didn't know what Dragon's Creek was. "It's a resort in the Smokies, near where Marlene and I are living. My company's negotiating to buy it, and the deal is very important. We used to own it, years ago—"

But he stopped, apparently reading her expression correctly. She had intended it to communicate how trivial she considered a business deal compared to a family member in need.

He changed his tack quickly. "Besides, she needs a woman. She needs someone to talk to."

"I'll be glad to call her—"

"An hour or two on the telephone won't help," he interrupted with the air of a man who'd anticipated the suggestion. "She needs company."

Hilary frowned, trying to fathom what he actually wanted. "Terri's leaving for college tomorrow," she said hestitantly. "She really couldn't—"

"Not Terri." He dismissed the idea immediately. "I was hoping you could come yourself."

"Me?" Hilary's voice rose, and several people nearby looked up curiously.

He nodded. "She needs you," he said, as though that explained everything.

Hilary pressed her lips together, infuriated by his offhand tone. She might have been a pizza he was ordering. No matter that they were, to all intents and purposes, total strangers. No matter that he was asking her to travel five hundred miles. No matter that she owned a business that might need tending to, that she had a home and obligations. No matter what. Her presence would be convenient, and therefore she should go.

It was ludicrous, really, and she would have laughed in his face if she hadn't been so concerned about Marlene.

"Miss Fairfax, please." As if on cue, he smiled again, trotting out the dimples. Hilary stiffened. Great. Now he was going to try charm. Too bad he didn't know she was immune to his kind of charm, the facile kind that came, not from the heart or from good character, but simply from having lucked out in the gene pool. That kind of charm affected some women like a drug, as addictive as it was destructive. Her mother had proved it years ago, and her sister was in a hearing room proving it right now.

But he didn't know that *this* Fairfax woman, at least, was immune, and he was still smiling. "Marlene wants you to come. And you *are* about to take your vacation, aren't you? The mountains are beautiful this time of year. Good change from this heat wave. It gets down into the forties at night."

She scowled. How did he find out she was about to take her vacation? Originally she hadn't planned to take one at all this year. Her company, a temporary-employment agency, had been neglected while she'd devoted herself to getting Terri back on her feet again. And the Halloween-Thanksgiving-Christmas stretch was starting in soon, the busiest time for employment agencies.

But she was tired, worn-out from worrying about her sister, and she needed a rest, so she'd decided to steal a two-week vacation. How had this man known that?

"Your secretary." He answered the unspoken question smoothly.

Hilary gave a mental groan. Her secretary shouldn't have told anyone, but apparently the girl wasn't as immune to charm as Hilary.

"It would only be for a couple of weeks," he said. "I won't be there much, and Marlene really needs some help. Quite honestly, I think she may be going off the deep end."

"Really?" Hilary bristled again. The deep end? What a condescending phrase! Disapproval lay in the set of his full lips, in the dark, downward slash of brow. He obviously found Marlene a trial.

To be fair, there had been moments during the years when Hilary herself had lost patience with Marlene. But she'd been careful enough—and kind enough— not to let it show. Marlene had not had an easy life.

"Can you be more specific, Mr. St. George?" She crossed her legs, pulling her slim green skirt down over her knees, then wished she hadn't. It was such defensive body language.

"The phrase 'going off the deep end,' while making your own attitude quite clear," she continued, "doesn't really illuminate Marlene's condition much, does it?"

"Doesn't it? I thought it was rather descriptive, actually. Let's see. She cries a lot." He began to tick off Marlene's symptoms. "She won't go out, sleeps all day and mopes all night. I think she's taking sleeping pills, though God knows where she gets them." He looked grim. "She could easily be putting the baby in jeopardy. I can't let her go on like this."

Hilary's muscles clenched involuntarily, sensing trouble. Marlene had had a turbulent childhood, losing her mother at only eleven and fighting so horribly with her father that she had run away from home five times before she was seventeen. The last time she had run to North Carolina, where she had met Tommy St. George. Hilary had hoped it was the beginning of better times for Marlene. Then Tommy had died, and Marlene was alone again.

"Is she sick?" Her worry had become a real anxiety. It sounded like much more than a passing depression. "Is she losing weight?"

"No. A little, maybe. I don't know." Conner's voice was clipped, implying that he didn't pay much attention to such things. Hilary felt her temper flare again. No wonder Marlene was unhappy.

"Maybe you could try a little harder to notice, Mr. St. George. Maybe all she needs is a little TLC."

He made a frustrated sound. "Come on, Miss Fairfax. This isn't something I can just cajole her out of. I told you how she's behaving."

"That's not unusual during pregnancy, especially for a woman who's also lost her husband in a tragic accident," Hilary said, controlling her voice with determination. He didn't care about Marlene. He was just trying to foist a difficult baby-sitting job off on someone else so that he could get back to his business. "You should be able to comfort her without calling in the marines. She's just a young, frightened woman. There's no reason to panic."

"No?" He gave a low growling sound and leaned forward. Up close, his eyes were bluer than she'd realized, less gray. "Well, how about this—"

At that moment, the hearing-room door opened, and Terri came tearing out, rushing toward Hilary, her face red and tense as if she'd been holding her breath.

"Honey!" Forgetting Conner, Hilary rose and stretched out her arms. Terri barely reached the haven of her sister's embrace before an explosion of sobbing burst from her.

"It was awful, Hilary," she cried, her words distorted by the tears. "They tried to make it sound like I was lying, and I . . . I . . ." The words grew too mangled to be understood.

"Shh, honey," Hilary soothed, gently stroking Terri's soft brown hair. Over her sister's bowed head she met Conner's eyes. He, too, had risen and stood silently watching the women, his face impassive. There was no way to tell what he thought. But from what he had said about Marlene, Hilary suspected he saw Terri as another hysterical woman about to "go off the deep end."

"We'll talk later," she said to him, the words coming out more harshly than she'd intended. She knew she couldn't abandon Marlene now. But some perverse streak in her didn't want to tell him that yet. Why not let him stew for a few hours? It would do him good to worry about somebody else for a while.

He started to speak, but she overrode his protests. "Later. Right now I'm taking my sister home."

CONNOR WAS DRIVING too fast. He always drove too fast when he was headed somewhere he didn't want to go, as if he had to get there before he could change his mind.

Catching himself, he eased his foot off the pedal, letting the BMW whine down to a more sedate speed. As he glanced in the rearview mirror to be sure that the driver behind him slowed, too, his reflection caught him by surprise. His dark glasses—only in Florida would he still need sunglasses at seven o'clock on a fall evening—hid his eyes, but his brow was furrowed and the corners of his jaw were hard, squared off by the tight clamp of his teeth.

Where the hell was all this tension coming from? He flexed his fingers slowly, peeling them one at a time from their stranglehold on the steering wheel. *Easy, partner. No one's forcing you to do this.* Out of the corner of his eye he glimpsed his coat lying on the seat beside him, one pocket distorted by the small box it held in its satin-lined cavern. Reaching over, he slipped his hand into the pocket and wrapped his fingers around the velvety box. He bounced it slightly in his palm, as though he could calculate the wisdom of his decision as scientifically as the jeweler had calculated the number of carats.

But of course he couldn't. In frustration his fingers squeezed the box until the velvet flattened, and an ache in his jaw warned him that he was clenching it again. No one was forcing him to do this. No one was forcing him to ask Tina Patterson to marry him. The little velvet box had been his own idea.

Why the hell did Tina live so far out in the suburbs? It gave him too much time to think. He didn't want to think anymore, didn't want to weigh and worry and deal with the annoying little voice that kept asking him if he was really in love with Tina.

He couldn't wait for true love, whatever that might be. He was ready to settle for true friendship, true commitment, true partnership. Damn it, he was lonesome, pure and simple. Was that so strange? It had been building, this nameless dissatisfaction with his life, for a long time, until it had reached a peak that was like a physical pain. Sex, the medicine prescribed by those of his friends who observed his solitary nights, was not the answer. Short-term flings had years ago become first a bore, then an ordeal and finally downright unendurable. Fed up to the teeth with the tragicomedy casual sex had become, he hadn't even slept with Tina, though he'd been seeing her for a year now.

It had taken Tommy's death, then Marlene's startling announcement that Tommy had left behind an unborn child, to give Conner's dissatisfaction a name. No wonder one-nighters weren't working. He didn't want a woman. He wanted a wife, a family, a home that wasn't just a glorified hotel room. He wanted to get married, and he wanted to do it before Marlene's baby was born.

But he didn't want to *think* the thing to death. If only Hilary Fairfax hadn't been so stubborn. If she had agreed to his offer right away, instead of arguing for an hour before refusing to even make a decision, this whole velvet-box thing would be a done deal.

Just the thought of Hilary Fairfax made his tension increase, the way a jackhammer would affect a headache. What had Marlene told Hilary about him, he wondered, to make her so antagonistic? The look in her eyes couldn't have been more unfriendly if he'd just robbed her at gunpoint.

Actually, there was no telling *what* Marlene might have said. Her emotions ricocheted around, bouncing off the walls like a ball in a game of squash. Maybe it was just the pregnancy, but she was damned unpredictable.

But why should he care what Hilary Fairfax thought, anyway? He had enough problems of his own. Such as, what exactly was he going to do about Tommy's baby? It was due in just two months, and he hadn't even broached the subject with Marlene. At the moment she was happy to hang around, supported in grand style by the St. George money, but eventually she'd want a home of her own.... And she'd be taking the baby with her.

That was unacceptable. So unacceptable it made him feel slightly wild even to think about it. In fact, he hadn't figured out yet what *was* acceptable about this whole wretched situation. But he'd work it out somehow—he had to. He was a born businessman, and he'd learned long ago that almost anything could be reduced to dollars and cents—particularly if you had *enough* dollars and cents and were dealing with someone like Marlene.

He flicked off his sunglasses. How could Tommy have married such a gold digger? How could it be that this nineteen-year-old spoiled brat had been given so much power over Conner's life, his happiness, his future?

And she used that power. Boy, did she use it! At first it had been an ambiguous, weeping hint about whether she could go through the pregnancy alone. That one sentence had secured her a place in Conner's home and all his financial protection. Once, when he had balked at some staggering bill or another, she had threatened to run away and put the baby up for adoption anonymously. Now it was this despondence, this emotional blackmail—make me happy, or the baby will suffer.

Oh, Tommy. Why a woman like this? But the question was, as always, unanswerable. Tommy couldn't tell him. Tommy was dead, drowned when the boat he'd been recklessly driving overturned. Tommy, who had not been wearing a life jacket . . .

Conner's heart began to pump wildly, as if he had just run a race, and he tried to shut out the thoughts. And the guilt—the unassuageable guilt he'd live with for the rest of his life. He tried to close the door in his mind. Save those thoughts for the middle of the night. Save them for the nightmares. . . .

He glanced at the little velvet box. What would Tina think about the nightmares? Blond and beautiful, she'd been raised to handle men the way Dan Marino handled a football. She was smart and she was sweet, as long as she didn't have to handle anything not covered in the pages of the Southern Belle Rule Book. Rule Number One was the most important—a belle's man must be a Man. Rule Number Two ranked way up there, too—her man must be rich.

Well, rich he could manage. As soon as he closed the Dragon's Creek Resort deal, American Leisure Company would be as big as ever, as big as it was before all the trouble. He owned resorts across North America, in every playground worthy of the name. Rich wasn't the problem.

And until three months ago, macho hadn't been a problem, either. "Cocky and confident," his father had always said to his two sons, half joking, half serious. "That's the way women like their men." And Conner, at least, hadn't disappointed him. Former football captain turned captain of business, a Southern deb's dream. Until Tommy's death.

Unconsciously he pressed the accelerator to the floor. The change didn't show on the outside—not yet. Conner snorted, a soft, self-derisive sound that could hardly be heard over the roar of the engine. What would the lovely Tina say if, one night while her rugged husband slept beside her on their satin sheets, he woke up howling and sweating, chased from his sleep by a nightmare?

He laughed out loud at the thought of Tina's discovering herself royally gypped, as indignant as if her beloved Porsche turned out to have a Ford engine, or her pretty diamond necklace turned out to be cut glass. The laugh dwindled to a mirthless chuckle. She'd definitely want her money back. Daddy would have to buy her a great big divorce to make her feel better.

But that wasn't really what would happen, and the realization made his smile disappear altogether. Tina wouldn't ever make a scene—she hated scenes. She'd just quietly despise him for his weakness and perhaps withdraw to a room of her own where she could pretend the nightmares didn't exist. A chill passed over his skin, though central Florida was in the grip of a heat wave.

The BMW took the last corner quickly, bringing the Patterson mansion into sight. Its bastardized Mediterranean architecture was at its best against the deep orange sky, and as usual, a half-dozen expensive sports cars clustered around the house like barnacles. Another party. Tina loved parties even more than she loved her Porsche. Certainly more than she would love a disappointing husband who cried in his sleep like a little boy.

He had a sharp, sudden image of Hilary Fairfax folding her sister into her arms, stroking and murmuring while buckets of tears flooded onto her shoulder. Her voice was more like musical notes than words. And her hands were so gentle, feathering over the girl's hair.

Something twisted inside him, something primitive and painful that felt like hunger, and he forced the image away. What kind of a fool was he? Did he think Hilary Fairfax would pat his head and tell him everything would be all right? He remembered the hard glint in her green eyes when she'd looked at him. Not bloody likely she'd have any sympathy to spare for him!

It didn't have a damned thing to do with Hilary Fairfax, but suddenly he knew he couldn't go into Tina's hulking mausoleum of a house. He whipped the BMW into a sharp U-turn, sending his sunglasses, coat and the little velvet box tumbling onto the floor, and headed away as fast as his accelerator would take him.

CHAPTER TWO

HILARY HAD THOUGHT she'd feel foolish. Bobby socks and poodle skirts at her age? Still, it was a great party. Somebody had spiked her Coke float so full of rum she'd probably be sick as a dog in the morning, but she felt wonderful tonight. Besides, she defied anyone to be depressed while Bill Haley and the Comets were singing "Rock around the Clock."

Her troubling day was receding nicely. Terri was in high spirits, her emotional storm behind her, hopefully for good. Hilary herself had almost forgotten the look of anger frozen on Conner St. George's face when she'd refused to give him an answer today. He could just *be* angry. Tomorrow would be time enough to tell him what she'd decided about Marlene.

She sent a mental thank-you to whichever mischievous coed had slipped the liquor into the float. It was definitely helping her shake the blues. In fact, one more drink and she'd be dancing with the college kids herself, auburn ponytail bouncing and stiff petticoat flashing, forgetting to feel silly.

And why not? Terri had begged her to dress up for her back-to-college fifties' bash, and Hilary would do anything for her, even throw herself in front of the proverbial train.

However, she thought as she dumped hundreds of malted-milk balls into a big plastic bowl, she'd never been able to imagine how that train trick could possibly help anyone.

"Squash you flat as a pancake, that's all," she said sagely to the candy as she finished her float and wiped off her ice-cream mustache. "What earthly use is a squashed-flat sister?"

"Is this a riddle?" Terri appeared in the doorway to the backyard, a tray of corn dogs propped on one hip and a teasing smile on her lips. Sudden tears pricked at Hilary's eyes. God, she loved Terri's smile. She'd been so afraid it had gone forever. "I give up," Terri said, shifting the tray to the other hip. "What earthly use *is* a squashed-flat sister?"

"Simple," Hilary answered, blinking back those quick tears. She didn't drink often—which was a good thing, if it turned her all maudlin and weepy. "It's easier to pack her in your suitcase and take her along with you to college." She took her sister's face in both hands and planted a kiss on the tip of her nose. "Know what, little pickle? I love, love, love you."

"I know," Terri said, setting down her tray. She hooked her hands over Hilary's forearms. "Me, too. But you've got to stay here, madly earning money for my tuition."

"Yeah, but I'll miss you." The tears just wouldn't go away. That was definitely going to be her last Coke float. "Really miss you."

Terri frowned lightly. "I'll be okay, Hilary." Without a word both their gazes fell to where Terri's sleeve had ridden back, revealing two long scars on the inside of her wrist.

Terri looked up first. "Really," she said insistently, dropping her arms so that her sleeve covered the mark. "I'll be fine. I'll have a thousand dates. I'll join two sororities. I'll go to every football game. I'll even join the team—"

"And you'll study." Hilary tried for a stern expression.

"Well," Terri said with mock reluctance. "If I have time."

Hilary shook her head, but she didn't speak. Just beyond the kitchen door, someone pushed a new set of buttons on the rented jukebox and an early Elvis hit exploded into the warm autumn air, making conversation impossible.

Hilary rolled her eyes and groaned. Someone had turned the volume up. Oh, she'd hear about this tomorrow.

But they were having so much fun! Hilary looked out to where the kids were dancing and laughing. Such good kids. They had stuck by Terri loyally this past year, calling and writing and visiting though they were away at college and Terri was still at home recovering. And now that Terri was finally able to join them, coming in a bit late in the term but full of eager optimism, they were so happy for her, so supportive.

For all of that, Hilary was very grateful. It made letting go a little easier. A little.

She resisted the urge to gather Terri in her arms and hug her until the worried ache in her heart disappeared. Instead, she hoisted the bowl of candy and nudged Terri toward the door. "Let's go feed the starving multitude."

But the multitude had other pleasures on their minds.

"All right, everybody," a young man called as someone else began punching buttons on the jukebox. "Limbo alert!"

It was a popular decision, met by much whistling and cheering. Two boys grabbed the long pole of the pool scrubber, holding it chest high. The others formed a line as the merry beat of "Limbo Rock" pounded the air around them. Dropping her tray on the outdoor bar, Terri skipped to the back of the line. "You, too, Hilary," she said, pulling her sister by the hand. "Let's see if all those hours at aerobics class were worth anything."

Hilary hung back, laughing. "I'm the chaperon," she said, trying to extricate herself. "I just watch."

"But it's fun!" Terri's voice was wheedling. "Please?"

The other kids added their voices. "Come on, Hilary," they cried with a lamentable lack of respect for her "advanced" years. She should have taught them to call her Ms. Fairfax and be quietly deferential.

Too late now, though. Before she could get stern, someone had whisked the bowl of candy out of her hands and pushed her to the front of the line. The boys held the bar in front of her nose, grinning while she made laughing noises of demurral that were blithely ignored. She felt hands at her back, pushing. And then in the distance, just barely, over the insistent beat of the music, she heard the sound of the doorbell.

Thank God. Saved by the—

"I'll get it," a young man hollered as he bolted indoors. "You don't want to lose your place in line, Hilary." And so she was stuck.

Once she relaxed and accepted her fate, it was rather fun. The first few passes were a breeze, then it got harder. The song played over and over on the juke-box, until her heart seemed to beat in sync with the rhythm. Lower and lower the bar went, until almost everyone had been eliminated. The few who were left had an enthusiastic audience. Roars of delight met every success; roars of laughter greeted each ignominious defeat.

Hilary's knees and thighs burned from the struggle to clear the bar without falling. Perspiration moistened her hairline and her clinging cotton-knit sweater seemed uncomfortably warm. Finally, on her last try, she bent so far back her ponytail dragged the ground, and the tips of her breasts just barely cleared the bar.

Knees aching, back feeling about to break, she knew she'd won. If only she could get her head under without losing her balance. The crowd was in a cheering frenzy, stamping, clapping and calling her name. But she couldn't quite manage the last two steps. Her balance was failing....

And as she brought her head up a little, thinking that maybe, just maybe, she would make it, she noticed the new spectator standing in front of her. She saw his gray slacks first, her eyes just at thigh-level.

Her horrified gaze rose quickly to the tough jaw and the ridiculous dimples.

Deep, deep dimples. Conner St. George wasn't politely smiling now. He was holding back an all-out, rip-roaring grin.

As she met his laughing blue eyes, her knees turned to water. And with that she fell flat on her rear.

Conner shouldn't have laughed. He tried not to. But Hilary Fairfax, who'd been so stern and unapproachable at the courthouse this afternoon, had a look of such utter shock on her face as she'd plopped helplessly onto her bottom that he couldn't stop himself. Unforgivable. He could only hope that his laughter would get lost in the general hilarity.

But who on earth would have believed she could be so *cute?* This afternoon he'd pegged her as one of those control junkies, well-educated, well-bred and uptight as hell. He knew lots of female executives—and males, too, for that matter—who fit that description. He appreciated their competence, but he didn't seek out their company after work.

Looking at her now, her skirt bunched high on her bare thighs, her face glowing with perspiration and embarrassment, he could hardly believe she was the same person.

She clambered to her knees and, busily smoothing her skirt with both hands, shot a furious glare his way, as though he'd personally invented gravity. He recognized the angry flash of those wide green eyes—oh, yes, this was the same woman. Such fire! She really hated being caught with her dignity down.

Trying to compose his face into an expression less inflammatory, he held out his hand. "Sorry to have interrupted your party," he said as soberly as possible. It was difficult, because his mouth kept trying to break into another smile. She looked so indignant, so like an angry little girl, with her baby-fine auburn hair spilling into her eyes and round spots of color high on her cheeks. "I have to go back to North Carolina tomorrow, and I wanted to talk again, maybe settle things tonight."

He could almost see her mentally pulling herself together. A couple of quick hard blinks, and the fire in her eyes was extinguished. A couple of deep breaths, and the stains on her cheeks faded. With a decent facsimile of cool dignity she took his hand, but she didn't really use it, relying, instead, on her own trim thighs to raise herself to a standing position.

She let go of it the millisecond she could. Her reaction probably couldn't be classified as rude, but it was clear he'd never make her top-ten list.

"All right, Mr. St. George," she said. Her voice didn't go with the ponytail and poodle skirt. It was definitely a tailored-suit voice. "Let's talk inside."

Conner could have sworn he felt a physical chill as she swept past. Wow—from fire to ice in ten seconds flat. He probably wouldn't even make her top-one-hundred list.

None of which mattered, he reminded himself as he followed the haughtily bouncing ponytail into the house, as long as she agreed to help him with Marlene.

The nerve of the man! Hilary rolled the sliding glass door open so forcibly it slammed against its track. What gave him the right to show up on her doorstep unannounced and unwelcome? Men like Conner St. George absolutely infuriated her, men who thought the whole world was their garden and tramped through....

With effort, Hilary halted her belligerent torrent of thoughts, uncomfortably aware that her embarrassment was making her overreact. He couldn't have known she was giving a party tonight. And maybe he really was worried about Marlene, though nothing he'd said this afternoon had given her that impression.

But, oh, what a fool she must have looked, legs splayed, skirt riding up. She could hardly stand to think about it.

She felt his eyes on her back as she led the way through the house. When she'd decorated she'd let her romantic side have free rein. Irish-lace curtains at the windows, voluptuous rose chintzes on the soft sofas, warm Early American pine everywhere, fresh flowers on the sideboard.

Seeing it now, she was sure he thought it downright schmaltzy. He was very much the chrome-and-elegance type, a minimalist who probably decorated with electronics and expensive modern art that someone else had picked out. The archetypical bachelor.

She hurried down the hall toward the den, which was the only room in the house formal enough to conduct business in. As they passed walls dense with old family photographs, he slowed, and she winced as he stopped completely to study one taken on her fourth birthday.

It was a particularly sentimental photo, with the gauzy, sun-dappled look of an Impressionist painting. She was standing in the tall grass, her yellow party dress billowing around her and her golden-red hair just a fine mist in the wind. She stared right into the camera, her wide eyes so open, so trusting. Of course, that was long before her family fell apart, long before she had learned not to trust anyone.

"Cute," Conner pronounced, not taking his eyes from the picture. His dimples were just barely visible, as though the photo amused him in some secret way he didn't intend to share. "Very cute."

"All four-year-olds are cute," she said curtly, holding the den door open, waiting for him to pass through first. "It's an immutable law of nature."

She thought she heard him chuckle, but it was so low she couldn't be sure. The den windows looked out onto the patio, where the party was still in full swing, and the sounds of rock and roll filtered in through the glass. Seating herself at her desk, she motioned to the corner armchair.

"You wanted to talk?"

He settled himself comfortably before he answered, letting his eyes roam, taking both the room's measure and hers. She was glad this room, at least, was businesslike.

When the silence had stretched out so long that she felt the beginnings of a fidget, he finally spoke.

"Last week," he said, his voice tight, as though he disliked saying the words, "Marlene threatened to kill herself."

Hilary's mouth fell open slowly. Stunned, she stared at him, noticing, as one sometimes does during moments of shock, trivial details. Those startling wings of silver at his temples. He was too young to be going gray, wasn't he? She tried to remember if Marlene had mentioned his age—thirty-three, maybe?

But that wasn't the point. He'd just said that... Forcing her numb lips shut, she tried to pull her skittering thoughts together.

"No! She couldn't have!" She spoke emphatically, as though she could will his sentence away. Marlene's letters had sounded unhappy after Tommy died, but hardly suicidal. Surely Hilary would have sensed anything that drastic.

"Yes." He leaned forward even farther, until his face was only inches from hers. "She did."

"Why?" Hilary could hardly get the word out. She seemed to have lost her breath. How *could* it be true? She had heard from Marlene only two weeks ago. "When?"

"About ten days ago." Ignoring her first question, he sat back in his chair and ran his hand over his hair, the first sign of stress she'd seen in him. "I don't think she really meant it, but even so..."

"Even so—" Hilary's voice was hoarse, and she cleared her throat "—any suicide threat should be taken seriously. It's a—" she cleared it again "—a cry for help." *And I should know,* she thought, clamping her lips together. *I should know.*

Conner nodded curtly. "Right. The situation is serious. This is my brother's child she's carrying, Miss Fairfax. If she tries to kill herself, then the baby—" He stopped, and Hilary watched the muscle in his jaw work. "I told you. I'm not asking you to come babysit a hysterical teenager because it's inconvenient for me to do it. She really needs you."

"She needs *someone,*" Hilary countered anxiously. "But she may need a professional, someone who's trained—"

"No," Conner interrupted, impatient again. "She refuses to see a therapist. She says she's only comfortable talking to you. I'm asking you because Marlene sees you as a friend. Besides, I hear you have some special experience with this kind of thing."

How had he had heard about that? Feeling the heat seep slowly into her cheeks, Hilary glanced angrily at him. What had Marlene told him? Not everything surely. Not those things that were too personal to tell.

But his eyes were knowing. Marlene *had* told him.

"Marlene and your sister were friends, weren't they?"

She nodded warily. She had expected a direct attack, a demand for capitulation. This serpentine approach surprised her. "Yes," she admitted. "They were good friends, as well as cousins. Marlene didn't have many girlfriends, but she liked Terri."

"They spent a lot of time together?"

"Yes." Hilary well remembered those days, back before Marlene had run away to North Carolina, back before her exotic elopement with Tommy St. George. Hilary had always worried about Marlene. She was so beautiful, so hungry for excitement, for love, for money, for men, and so aware that her beauty could obtain those things for her. But she'd also been naive and endearingly candid about her dreams. "She didn't have anyone else, really. Her mother was dead, and Marlene and her father didn't get along."

"Did you like her?"

Hilary frowned. What was he getting at? "Of course," she said hotly. "I told you. She's like a second sister to me."

"She likes you, too." He lifted his leg, resting his ankle on his knee, and leaned back. "But tell me. Did it ever occur to you that your sister's suicide attempt might have planted the same idea in Marlene's mind?"

At first Hilary just gaped, unable to believe what she'd heard. Then, very slowly, like a stain spreading across tightly woven cloth, his words sank in. Frowning, she cast a worried glance over her shoulder. Could Terri have heard him?

No. The kids weren't paying any attention to them. Reassured, she transferred her gaze to Conner and tried to decide what to say. How dared he blame Terri for Marlene's problems? Since the suicide attempt a year ago, Terri had been through so much—and she already carried enough guilt over what she'd done. She didn't need more.

"It certainly did not!" Hilary responded vehemently. She sounded furious, and she didn't care. "Is that what you think?"

"I don't know." He sounded reasonable, controlled, and irrationally she wanted to slap him. He ought to be angry. He ought to be frightened. "I think it's possible."

"Why?" She licked her lips, though they weren't dry, needing an excuse to unclench her jaw.

"Little things, really," he said musingly. "She talks about you and Terri a lot. And I think she envies how close you are, how you've devoted yourself to taking care of Terri." He sighed, as though weary of the whole mess. "And frankly, she wouldn't be the first person to try all the wrong things to attract attention."

Hilary couldn't deny any of it. The extra love and support she'd showered on Terri since her tragedy had probably been noticed by Marlene. Noticed and envied.

In fact, it was during the worst of things that Marlene had run away to North Carolina. And, though she'd been in touch frequently through letters and calls, Marlene hadn't returned to Florida since. That was why Hilary had never even met Tommy or his brother, Conner.

And maybe it made sense that Marlene's SOS should come now. With Terri going off to college, Marlene might have hoped that Hilary would have some time and love to spare for her. Poor Marlene, always on the outside, wanting to come in and be loved.

But wasn't Conner missing something more obvious? Since, with his accusation, he hadn't bothered to spare her feelings, Hilary decided not to sugarcoat her own words. Why should he escape the blame he was so eager to dispense?

"Are you sure," she said with deceptive blandness, "that it's *my* attention she was trying to get?"

Conner scowled. "Meaning?"

"Meaning, couldn't she be trying to get *your* attention? Wouldn't that be more natural in the circumstances?"

He shook his head. "No," he said flatly. "She already has mine. She's carrying my brother's child, remember?"

"Maybe she wants more than your interest in the child," Hilary suggested. "You're quite important in her life right now, you know. You may even remind her of Tommy."

He made a sudden motion. "That's absurd! I'm *nothing* like my brother."

Hilary's inner antennae quivered, alerted by the unwarranted heat in his voice. Why was he reacting so vehemently to that innocent suggestion? She began to wish she had known Tommy. "Still, it seems possible that Marlene might be hoping—"

"She's not," he interrupted roughly. "She knows what I think of her. She knew I didn't approve of Tommy's marriage."

"Did you think he was too young?" Tommy St. George had been twenty-two, old enough to seem glamorous to the eighteen-year-old Marlene, but rather young to be taking on the responsibilities of a wife and child. Certainly too young to die.

"Too young, too spoiled, too immature, too head-strong, too everything." His mouth was tight, his voice deep with censure, and he looked just beyond her, as if seeing into a troubling past that was still real to him. "I disapproved of Tommy marrying, yes. But more specifically I disapproved of Tommy marrying *her*. He needed a tight rein, someone to keep him in line, but Marlene was just as bad as he was. Maybe worse. Between them they didn't have the sense to scramble eggs." He brought his gaze back to meet hers. "It was an unacceptable marriage, doomed from the start."

The note of untempered anger she heard shocked her, and she pressed back against her chair, as though his contempt was a blowtorch she must evade. She realized suddenly that Marlene had been right. Conner despised her and didn't bother to hide it. In that moment, with Conner's hard eyes on her, with his words heating the air in her little den, she knew nothing on earth could keep her from going to North Carolina.

"I'll go," she said rashly, before she could change her mind. "It sounds as if Marlene could use a friend."

CHAPTER THREE

FOR CONNOR, returning to his house in Dragon's Creek, North Carolina, was as close to coming home as anything he'd ever known. Even Marlene's pouting presence couldn't spoil it. As soon as he passed the town limits and headed up the mountain, he felt a distinct lightening of spirits. A familiar canopy of oaks, silver maples and pines arched over his head protectively. He was almost there.

And not a moment too soon. He'd been driving for hours. His back was aching. Gratefully, he pulled up the steep driveway that led to his house and angled the car around for a more secure berth.

He didn't get out. The sunset had been a stunner, pouring a deep orange light onto the trees, intensifying their fall colors. But it was fading now, softening into a peaceful montage of blacks and grays.

The Smoky Mountains—more specifically, the Dragon's Creek Resort in the Smoky Mountains—was the most beautiful land in the world, and it rolled out like a tapestry from his own front door. At any season, in any light, it was a sight that never failed to please him. He could hardly wait to buy it back. He wanted to be able to sit here every night and look out and know that it all belonged to him again.

With a small electric hum, the windows rolled down, letting in the sharp, clean air of a mountain twilight. Killing the engine, he slouched in his seat, resting his head against the leather cushions. He watched the mountains as passively as he might have watched a movie, enjoying the profound absence of humanity, the timeless grace of the rounded peaks as they faded into the gathering dusk.

God, he was tired. He'd driven straight through, unwilling to leave his car behind in Florida, yet afraid to leave Marlene alone for another day. Afraid. The word jangled, foreign and unpleasant to his internal ear. It wasn't a word he was accustomed to using about himself.

Which was why he was so tired. Fear, he discovered, was exhausting. He blinked, realizing he could easily fall asleep here. And maybe, with the timeless lullaby of night birds and windswept trees to soothe him, he might sleep the whole night through. Letting his eyes drift shut, he wondered vaguely whether people more familiar with fear found it less enervating.

He honestly couldn't remember being afraid before. Until his uncle had lost the Dragon's Creek Resort, putting the whole American Leisure Company in jeopardy, life had been so easy, following some unseen but unchanging script that seemed to result in endless success and happiness.

And even after his uncle's mishandling of the family business, Conner had known only anger and determination, never fear. He had *known* he could put American Leisure back on track. Actually, it had been rather thrilling, like going into the locker room at halftime with your team behind twenty-one to nothing and *knowing* you could still win the game.

He shifted, trying to ease the pain in his back. It didn't go away. But he could handle the pain. It was the fear he couldn't take. The fear and the damned nightmares.

He sat up with a jerk and shoved the door open. Why couldn't he see all this as just another challenge, another game to win? He had to find a way to get back into the script he was born to play. Maybe after he closed the deal that would make Dragon's Creek his again…maybe after Tommy's baby was born…maybe then the nightmares would go away.

It unnerved him, sometimes, to see how much he was depending on this baby to make everything right. He was too mature, too practical—wasn't he?—to believe that anything could provide a miracle cure for life's ills. And besides, becoming dependent on the thought of the baby left him, by definition, dependent on Marlene for this miracle, on her childish, selfish whims and emotional vagaries.

It was time to go in. Janie, his housekeeper, had left for the day, and Marlene hated being alone. He hoped she wasn't in one of her weepy moods. Or, God forbid, in one of her sulky moods, in which she refused to speak to him all through dinner, ostentatiously reading a murder mystery and sniffing occasionally to show she was nursing a secret and probably imaginary grudge.

He picked up his briefcase, exhaling a breath that condensed and hung in the cooling air briefly like a question mark. Well, it didn't matter whether she was into Kleenex or Christie, because he had good news.

Hilary Fairfax, thank God, would be here in the morning.

IT WAS ACTUALLY MIDDAY before she got there. She'd driven Terri to Gainesville on Saturday and left her at the dorm with much hugging, laughing and weeping on both sides. It was so hard to let go. Hilary's ride back to Winter Park was grim and silent.

Perhaps it was a good thing she had to rush off to North Carolina the very next day. It left little time for brooding, and as soon as she got off the airplane in Asheville and glimpsed the mountains, still mostly green but dotted here and there with yellow and cinnamon, she began to feel almost lighthearted. It was beautiful country, and the clear, frosty air was a welcome change after Florida's muggy heat.

It was almost like being on a real vacation. She hadn't had one in so long she'd forgotten how therapeutic a change of scenery could be. Her little rental car chugged happily up the mountains, following Conner's extremely precise directions.

Two-point-four miles past the second scenic overlook, she turned left into a half-hidden private drive. From there, seven curving tenths of a mile to the house.

Up she climbed, winding through wonderful old trees and granite formations that winked and sparkled in the afternoon sunlight. Somewhere she heard water gurgling, occasionally swelling into rippling laughter and sometimes getting lost altogether. Once a surprising bank of foxglove, at least three feet high and still heavy with white clusters, rose in front of her as the drive took a sharp twist to the left.

And finally there was the house. She didn't see it until she was practically on top of it, so perfectly did it blend with its environment. Though quite modern and obviously expensive, hiding there in the forest, it was somehow as quaint and magical as a fairy-tale cottage.

Made from the same woods that towered over it, the house was a series of irregular tiers, one spilling into the next with porches that were cut out around massive tree trunks and balconies that dripped with voluptuous hanging plants. It looked, she decided, more like a waterfall than she'd have thought any solid object ever could.

As her gaze slowly took it all in, she realized it was huge. On each floor—there appeared to be three, or was it four?—whole walls were made of glass, reflecting the woods so clearly that the house seemed to have absorbed the trees and sky into itself.

Above all, the house gave off a feeling of serenity. She thought of how Terri would love it, how easy it would be for a wounded psyche to heal itself here. This house had been built with an understanding of cosmic things, things like peace and harmony, endurance and acceptance. Things that were so much bigger than the petty grievances of the modern rat race.

She breathed deeply, as if trying to drink of that enduring peace. She was glad, so glad, she had come.

But suddenly the peace was broken.

Somewhere in the unseen depths of the house a door slammed. Hilary opened her eyes in time to see Marlene come barreling out to stand on the lowest balcony, fury emanating from her entire body as she faced the house.

"I hate you!" Marlene shrieked, her voice high and shrill, carrying like the cry of a fierce bird. "You don't care about me. You don't even care about the baby. All you care about is yourself, and I hate you, Conner St. George."

Her voice wavered, and she crumbled to the wooden floor, hanging on to the railing and burying her face in her arms. "I hate you," she sobbed. "I hate you."

Hilary shot from the car and took the steps two at a time. She reached Marlene, gathering the weeping girl into her arms just as Conner St. George came onto the porch. Her heart racing from the shock of the scene, Hilary glanced up at him accusingly, then bent over Marlene's huddled form.

"What's going on here?" she said, concern for her cousin overshadowing everything else. "What have you done?"

She stroked Marlene's hair, then looked at Conner again, waiting for an answer. But he didn't speak. Their eyes locked. Hers were worried and reproachful, and his...

His were what? As she stared at him, a strange word flickered through Hilary's mind. Desolate. She thought she'd never seen a man look so desolate.

MARLENE'S TEARS finally dried, and she sat, stone-faced, on the bed in her room, plucking at the satin quilt. Her silky blond hair had miraculously remained unmussed, and even during the fury of her weeping, she'd been careful to wipe away any drizzling mascara. Consequently, Hilary noted with some amusement, misery was quite becoming to Marlene. With a great sigh, Marlene leaned against the headboard, lacing her fingers across the mound of her stomach. She was big for—Hilary tried to figure quickly—six months, though that wasn't unbecoming, either. It accentuated the delicacy of her slim arms, her trim legs.

"He's a sadist, Hilary. He really is. He won't give me any of Tommy's money, and it's just because he loves to see me suffer."

Hilary, who had been sitting on the edge of the bed hugging and soothing Marlene while she cried, moved to an armchair in the corner. "Come on, Marlene, isn't that a little melodramatic?"

Marlene pulled at the quilt again, almost viciously. "No, it isn't. He wants me to be his prisoner, to beg for everything. Every bite I eat, every stitch of clothing on my back. Everything."

Hilary's eyes swept around the large, lovely room, obviously newly decorated. Blue satin linens, flowered curtains, a vanity piled high with bottles and jars of expensive cosmetics—hardly a prison. And Marlene herself, dressed in a beautiful royal-blue maternity dress that proclaimed itself pure silk with every thread, hardly looked like a poor mistreated orphan. But Hilary knew that money was only one of the ways you could be required to pay for things. You could also pay for your pretty dresses with subservience, with a helpless dependence that was galling to an independent spirit. And the same person who generously dispensed silks and trinkets with one hand could well be doling out cruelty with the other. Her father had been like that, giving her mother everything in the world she could want materially, but absolutely nothing emotionally. It was like handing your credit card to a man dying of thirst in the desert and saying you'll be back in a couple of days.

Fortunately Marlene wasn't waiting for Hilary to respond. She bunched her eyelet-covered pillows behind her back and raged on.

"He never takes me out. He's gone half the time, anyway. All he ever does is go to meetings about buying back Dragon's Creek, or talk on the telephone about buying back Dragon's Creek, or if I'm very lucky, talk to *me* about buying back Dragon's Creek. Like I care. He must own a million resorts—what's the big deal about the one right next door? I mean, it's pretty, but..."

She lifted grieved blue eyes to Hilary. "I swear, Hilary, I'm nothing but a brood mare to him. He doesn't notice me as a person. It's never how am I feeling—it's always how's the baby. It doesn't mean anything to him that I'm Tommy's widow. My only claim to any consideration is that I'm Tommy's baby's mother." Her voice trembled again. "If anything happened to this baby, I'd be out on the streets so fast—"

Hilary interrupted the flow of complaint, which was clearly building toward a melodramatic crescendo. "We're not going to let anything happen to the baby. And besides, whatever his motives are, a sense of duty, or—"

"Sadism," Marlene interjected petulantly.

"Or sadism or whatever, at least he's willing to support you until the baby's born. That's what counts, isn't it?"

"I guess." Marlene didn't sound very definite. "But what about after?"

Hilary didn't have an answer for that. It was a question that had already occurred to her—what about after? Did Conner really imagine the three of them living here, together, Conner, Marlene and the baby? Or did he just hope for generous visiting rights, by virtue of his being Uncle Moneybags?

"I wouldn't be surprised," Marlene said bitterly, "if he tries to buy me off. You know, to buy the baby from me."

Hilary was shocked, and she glared at Marlene, hoping to calm the theatrics. "Well, *I* would be! That's ridiculous!"

"Is it?" Marlene eyed her cousin narrowly, apparently not as horrified as Hilary. "I wonder. I wonder how much he'd offer?" Then she sighed. "But it's

Tommy's money, anyway, isn't it? I don't understand why Conner has to dribble it out to me a dollar at a time. And he could at least be nice about it."

Hilary fought the urge to groan. She'd only been here an hour. She couldn't be growing impatient with Marlene already. Besides, it did seem strange. Shouldn't Marlene, as Tommy St. George's widow, have inherited whatever Tommy had owned? She made a mental note to find out. Conner probably wouldn't appreciate her prying, but she couldn't be much help to Marlene if she didn't know how things stood.

"Nice would be lovely," she said judiciously. "But remember, you can't change him. You can't change anyone but yourself. And your job right now is to get ready for this baby." She picked up the Lamaze manual that lay on the bedside table and leafed through it tranquilly, trying to communicate some calm. "When is the baby due?"

In spite of Hilary's efforts, Marlene seemed to become even more agitated. Without answering, she hoisted herself off the bed and paced to the window, staring out with the frustrated longing of a prisoner staring through the bars of her cell.

What now? Putting the manual down, Hilary joined her at the window, though she could see nothing out there that appeared distressing. It was a particularly lovely view, with an amber shaft of sunlight driving through a break in the trees, touching, like Midas, leaves, bark and stones alike.

Marlene probably didn't even see the golden beauty before her. She was silent, her body rigid. It occurred to Hilary that, deep in her heart, Marlene might be dreading the arrival of this baby—dreading the pain of delivery, the staggering responsibility of an infant, the permanent loss of her own carefree youth. A human reaction, quite natural, and yet one that probably appalled most new young mothers.

"Hasn't the doctor given you a date?"

"December tenth," Marlene said without turning to look at Hilary. Her voice was strangled, as if she found the words difficult to pronounce.

And there was the answer to Hilary's real question. A simple one of math. Tommy St. George and Marlene had been married for only three short months before his tragic death three months ago. Add to that the two months that stretched between today and December tenth, and you came up with eight months. This child had been conceived before Marlene and Tommy had married.

It didn't seem all that much, in this age of enlightenment, to be so miserable about, but Hilary knew from her experience with Terri that teenagers could take things very hard. Though she felt a surge of relief and a mental, *Oh, is that all?*, she didn't allow herself even a small smile. She put her arm around Marlene's shoulders and squeezed gently.

"Perfect," she said firmly. "Just enough time to do some serious shopping for baby clothes."

Marlene's shoulders didn't relax. "I can't go shopping," she said, her voice low and petulant. "His

Highness hasn't given me any money, remember? I guess he wants his only niece or nephew to go around wrapped in old kitchen rags.''

Feeling the cool, expensive silk of Marlene's maternity dress under her palm, Hilary couldn't help thinking that statement was unfair. Conner certainly hadn't made his sister-in-law go around in rags. Perhaps he'd expected Marlene to spend less on herself and more on the baby.

But obviously Marlene was in no mood to listen to reason. "I'll talk to him," Hilary promised, trying not to let her voice show how little she relished the thought of such an encounter. "Maybe we can get him to spring for a romper or two.''

But by the time Hilary left Marlene, who had curled up on the big soft bed for a nap, Conner was gone.

Hilary welcomed the opportunity to explore the house on her own. Suitcase in hand, she wandered through the large, airy rooms with a sense of surprise. Nowhere in the house did she see the ghastly glass-and-chrome bachelor decor she'd been expecting. The furniture was mostly wood, with just enough overstuffed sofas and chairs to give a feeling of comfort. Lush green plants peeked from every corner and, combined with the huge windows, seemed to bring the outdoors in. A fire had been laid in the main room, and it crackled comfortingly. It was a drowsy, contented, glad-to-be-safe-at-home fire. Hilary had a sudden, intense longing to grab a book from one of the built-in cases and curl up on that green corduroy armchair.

But first she had to find her room. The various levels were connected by small sets of steps, the rooms spilling into one another much as the balconies on the exterior did. Marlene had said Hilary's room was on the third floor, at the back of the house, and Hilary found it easily. While not as large as Marlene's room, it was still luxurious and charming.

Dropping her suitcase on the stand provided, she headed straight for the connecting bathroom, eager to wash off the travel grime and get into some fresh clothes. She cast one last look out the picture window and down onto the stream that burbled just beyond her balcony, and tried to quell the guilty feeling that was building inside her.

It was such beautiful country. Such a beautiful house. And such a luxurious bathroom! She bent over the marble tub, unbuttoning her sweater with one hand and twisting the faucet with the other.

Marlene's emotional state wasn't as serious as she had feared. Much as she hated to admit it, Conner had probably been right: her cousin's suicide threat had only been a ploy to get Hilary up here. Surely, then, she thought, breathing in the perfumed steam of the bubble bath as hot water roared from the tap, it wasn't wrong to enjoy herself just a little.

CONNOR LET HIMSELF into the darkened house almost furtively, aware that he desperately wanted to avoid an encounter with Marlene. It had been a tough night at a frustrating meeting, and he didn't trust himself to be patient with her right then.

He poured himself a stiff scotch, poked at the last pale red embers in the fireplace to settle them for the night and then walked through the darkness to his office. It was very late, but still too early to hope for sleep. Especially after that damned meeting.

How in hell had word leaked out that he was behind the offer to buy Dragon's Creek? He tossed back the last gulp of his drink and refilled it from the decanter in his office bar. He'd have somebody's head for it. The asking price had doubled once the Dragon's Creek people had discovered they were dealing with him.

They knew it wasn't just another deal to him. They knew his company had once owned Dragon's Creek Resort, and then lost it. They knew he was emotionally invested. They knew they *had* him.

The liquor wasn't helping. He shoved the glass away irritably, the whiskey rocking in the small glass and splashing onto the wooden bar. He knew he ought to abandon the deal now. A cardinal rule of business was *Don't get involved.* There was no room for superstition, revenge, sentimentality or any other emotional baggage.

His father's motto had always been *Keep your head on straight and keep your heart out of it.* Conner must have heard that sentence a hundred times. That had been his uncle's mortal sin. He hadn't been able to keep his heart out of it.

So Conner knew he should back out. The Dragon's Creek people thought he was a hooked fish, and they were going to try to reel him and all his money right into their hands. A smart fish would let go of the bait and wriggle free. A dumb fish would hang on, driving the hook deeper....

Damn! Marlene must have put the thermostat up to a hundred degrees. He couldn't breathe in here. Dragging his tie down from his throat, he shrugged out of his coat and opened the French doors.

The blast of cold air was bracing. Sobering, though he hadn't even realized he needed it. He tried to remember how many drinks he'd had at the dinner meeting and couldn't. Which meant it was too many. For punishment, he stepped onto the balcony. Immediately the wind rushed at him, slipping icy tentacles under his collar, between his buttons, inside his cuffs. He felt his skin shiver and tighten.

"Mr. St. George?"

At first he couldn't figure out where the voice was coming from. The moon was swaddled in clouds, and there was no artificial lighting on the balcony. The few spotlights he'd installed were trained up into the leafy crowns of nearby trees, glorifying the natural rather than the man-made.

But finally, even in the dim light, he found her. Hilary Fairfax stood maybe eight feet away, though she was technically on the balcony above him. He had forgotten, when he'd chosen that guest room for her, how close she'd be to his own quarters.

She bent over the balustrade, her long hair swinging over her shoulders to dangle above him. She was wearing something soft and flowing, high at the neck and falling down to her ankles and over her wrists. He couldn't quite tell what color it was, but it looked velvety and vaguely Elizabethan.

"Mr. St. George?" She tilted her head, and the light from her room caught one side of her face, exposing the pale curve of her cheek where it met the dark shadow of her eye. He could see only the outer corner of her mouth, but it seemed wistful, full, as though from weeping or kissing.

For what seemed an eternity, he stood there, staring up like some mooning Romeo while his body stirred in a response that was not vague in the least. The involuntary arousal annoyed him. Had his recent celibacy really left him in this pathetic state—as eager as a teenager, turned on by any woman who just happened to have sexy lips and a Juliet nightgown?

And a woman who didn't even like him, to boot. He remembered all too well how harsh and accusing those soft, shadowy eyes had been this afternoon. "What have you done?" she had asked, taking his culpability for granted. She'd already cast him as the bad guy.

Well, fine. If that was what it took to keep Marlene happy, he could stand it. Let Hilary Fairfax hate him. He had no intention of trying to have a sloppy one-night stand with Marlene's cousin, anyway. None at all.

But apparently his body wasn't listening to him, and his annoyance deepened. He looked up, unsmiling.

"Don't you think we can move to first names? If we're going to be living together, all that formality could get pretty tiresome." His voice sounded as cold as the air, and he was glad. At least she wouldn't be able to guess at the ridiculous heat that flickered in him.

"All right." She stood up straight, and her face became obscured by her hair. "Conner. I'm glad to see you're still awake."

He managed not to laugh at her innocent understatement. It was only one in the morning. He couldn't remember when he'd last gone to bed this early. Much less to sleep. "Really?" he said with an ironic twist to his voice. "Why is that?"

"I was hoping we could talk."

He made a phony display of checking his watch, which he couldn't begin to read in the darkness. *"Now?"*

She nodded. He could see the light sliding across the copper silk of her hair. "I'd like to," she said politely. "If you're up to it. I think it would be better to talk while Marlene's asleep."

"Fine." He shrugged. "In my office, then?"

She nodded again.

"Do you want me to come and get you—lead you down?"

She shook her head, her face flashing in, then out of the light. "I can find it," she said and moved away from the balcony, through the French doors that led to her room.

He was glad of the reprieve, however short. He needed time to collect himself. It must be the damned cold air, teasing his skin, making him feel all prickly and sharply aware of her. He went inside, slamming the door shut behind him.

Another drink, maybe. Numb would be nice.

CHAPTER FOUR

THE MINUTE SHE SAW HIM, Hilary wished she'd waited until morning. He looked desperately tired and unaccountably cross. His tie was loose and askew, as though he'd yanked it down with angry fingers. Wrinkles zigzagged across his white dress shirt, and the cuffs were unbuttoned and rolled up, exposing forearms well-muscled and dusted with dark hair.

Worse yet, though she hadn't noticed it in the dim light of the balcony, she could tell he'd been drinking. And judging from the glint in his eyes, he wasn't a happy drunk. Not, she thought, the most auspicious moment to ask for baby rompers.

But it was too late to back out now. He'd left the office door open, and when she entered the room he was already tucked in behind his big desk, as if to imply that she'd interrupted important business. She doubted that. The desk's surface was clear. She'd be willing to bet the only work he'd been doing was on the contents of that decanter she saw sitting on the bar.

He didn't even stand up when she came in, simply motioned her to sit with a wave of the glass in his right hand.

"This is about Marlene, I assume?"

"Yes." Hilary sat on the straight-backed chair in front of the desk, feeling a little like someone applying for a loan, which no doubt was exactly how he wanted her to feel. "Of course."

"Of course." He shifted in his seat with a heavy sigh, letting the glass dangle from his fingers as though he'd forgotten it was there. "You've had a chance to talk to her?"

She nodded. "We spent the whole evening together. Naturally we talked."

"Not so natural around here." He obviously hadn't forgotten his drink and, grimacing, tossed back the last of it. "Marlene can sit in the same room with me for hours without saying a word. She's a master of the cold shoulder. I think our record is just under four hours."

Hilary didn't know how to respond to that. She shifted in the stiff chair, suddenly aware of how chilly the room was. He must have been standing on the balcony with the doors open for a long time. Surreptitiously she rubbed at the gooseflesh that prickled along her arms.

His tone didn't improve the temperature much. Why was he telling her this? Did he expect her to apologize for Marlene's moods? Well, she wasn't going to. At this point she wasn't sure whose behavior was responsible for the stony silences he described. "That must be uncomfortable for both of you," she said, deciding to take the middle ground. "It sounds lonely."

He set the glass down slowly. "It is." Hitching one long leg up over his other knee, he leaned back in the leather chair, which creaked slightly as it accommodated his shifted weight.

"But I'm a hotel man," he added with a smile so shallow the dimples hardly showed at all. "I'm used to living with people I don't know, don't like and don't ever speak to."

For the second time in their short interview, Hilary felt unable to respond. What was she supposed to say? Delivered without a hint of pathos, his grim statement defied any attempt at courteous sympathy. Besides, she probably fell into the category of "don't know, don't like" acquaintances. Had he intended to be rude? His expression was too enigmatic to give her any clue. No wonder Marlene didn't talk to him, she thought irritably. It was strenuous work—an exercise in reading between the lines.

"So." He pulled at his tie until the knot separated, then slid it through his collar with a rustle of silk. "How did it go? I suppose she spent the evening listing all my flaws?"

"Oh, not all of them." Hilary was tired of tiptoeing through this conversational minefield. If she had any hope of helping Marlene, she had to stand up to Conner. Though he might find Marlene easy to bully, he wasn't dealing with an immature nineteen-year-old now, and it was time he recognized that. "She went alphabetically, and we only got as far as *D* tonight."

He was clearly surprised. Brows raised, he tossed the tie onto the desk, where it lay like a coiled snake between them. He stared at her curiously, obviously reassessing her. She sat rigidly erect, but beneath that appraising gaze her defiance ebbed, and a shiver ran through her. Had she gone too far?

"*D,*" he said, toying with the tie absently. "Let's see . . . she probably didn't say delightful."

Under the quiet words Hilary heard the subtle trickle of humor, and her stomach relaxed. She sat back in her chair and breathed again. "No, probably not."

"Or dashing?"

She shook her head.

"Hmm. More like . . . disagreeable?"

"Well." Hilary bit back a smile. "She started there."

He tilted his head to one side. "Domineering?"

"The word was mentioned." She couldn't help noticing that his eyes, which glinted as they caught the gleam from the desk lamp, were a smoky silver now.

"Degenerate, despicable and disgusting?" The dimples had appeared again on either side of his wide mouth, just deep enough to hold a fingertip. Probably every woman he'd ever dated found an excuse to touch those dimples. Hilary pushed her hands into the pockets of her robe. "Oh, I wouldn't go that far," she said, smiling finally at the absurdity of it. "Degenerate and despicable, perhaps, but not disgusting."

The man was fishing, of course, a typical masculine ploy. He knew that Marlene, even at her most petulant, couldn't find him disgusting. No woman could. And how did he manage to give the impression of amusement without actually smiling? Heavens, he was handsome. Disturbingly handsome. Yes, that was a *D* word that applied to Conner St. George. Disturbing.

At that moment the heating system switched on. A blast of warm air fluttered the ends of her long, loose hair up against her face, tickling at her chin and mouth. The strands caught on the dampness of her open lips.

Slowly, Conner's eyes fell to her mouth and remained fixed there, as though he was mesmerized by the gentle waving of the auburn wisps. Her fingers felt curiously clumsy as she pulled the hair free. Under his intense scrutiny, her lips tingled, and suddenly the room was much too hot. She felt herself flushing.

Defensively she pressed her lips together. This was ridiculous. She wasn't here to exchange electrically charged glances with Conner St. George. The conversation had taken an inappropriately coy turn, and it was time to get back to business. The last thing in the world she wanted was for him to think she was flirting.

"Actually, I believe Marlene is feeling rather oppressed right now," she said, firming her lips and fighting down the flush. "For someone as spirited as Marlene, this much dependence, however well-intentioned the master, chafes."

"Oppressed? By what?" His dimples flattened out, as did his voice. The laughter was gone. "Or should I say by *whom?*"

"By life." Hilary refused to let his change of tone disappoint her. Maybe he, too, was pulling back, realizing their repartee had become too chummy. Or maybe he just didn't like being criticized. "By finding herself alone and dependent. She's feeling—" she groped for a word "—downtrodden."

For a instant Conner's eyes narrowed to cold slivers of silvery light, and then he stood up and turned toward the bar. Throttling the decanter with one large fist, he splashed more whiskey into his empty tumbler.

"Now there's a *d*-word for you," he said, his back to her. "Downtrodden. And I suppose the footprints on her back are supposed to be mine?"

"Of course not," she said, trying to sound sensible and unemotional, though her heart jumped nervously as she watched him tilt his head and drain the glass again. Hadn't he had enough to drink? It would be impossible to reason with him if he got truly drunk. "It's just that if you let her have a little more independence, maybe she'd—"

"Independence?" He wheeled around, the glass still clenched in his hand. His knuckles were white, and for a moment she feared the crystal would splinter under such a fierce grip. "That's such a stock euphemism, Hilary. I'm disappointed. Why don't you just come straight out and say it? Marlene doesn't want independence. She wants money."

Hilary's mouth opened for an impulsive denial, but he cut into her stumbling syllables.

"Yes, she does. That's what she wants, and that's *all* she wants."

"That's not true," she said, continuing to strive for a calm tone.

"Oh, really?" He put his glass down on the desk and raised one skeptical brow. "Didn't she send you to me to ask for money?"

"Yes, but—"

She broke off. Conner had made a disgusted sound. Gesturing dismissively, he dropped back into his chair and proceeded to study his glass, as though he considered her admission a conclusion to the discussion.

But Hilary wasn't caving in that easily. "No. She didn't *send* me. It was my own idea to talk to you...."

She couldn't tell if he was even listening. He stared into his glass as intently as if the secrets of the universe were written in its amber depths. "Conner," she began again, her tone placating, though her temper had risen to the danger level. She had to control it. If she wasn't careful, things might end up being worse than ever for Marlene. "She just wants what all new mothers want. She wants to be able to buy clothes and pretty things for her baby. It's such an exciting time for a woman...."

Conner glanced up.

"Oh, baloney," he said, but he sounded exhausted, and for the first time she heard a hint of a slur in his tired voice. "Marlene married Tommy for his money. Her problem is that she can't accept that her meal ticket has expired."

Her meal ticket? Hilary almost choked as she tried to swallow and gasp at the same time. "That's enough!" She leapt to a standing position, nearly knocking over the chair as outraged loyalty shot through her. "That's the most insulting thing I've ever heard. And if you weren't disgustingly drunk you wouldn't have dared say it.''

He smiled, but it was an unpleasant smile, and the dimples didn't surface. ''So. We've added 'disgusting,' after all.'' Raising his chin, he stared up at her. From that angle, with distorted, exaggerated shadows, his face was a stranger's. ''You're probably right—sober, I wouldn't have said it. But drunk or sober, spoken or unspoken, it would still be true.''

Letting his head fall against the chair, he closed his eyes. ''Poor Tommy. He was such an easy mark.'' His eyelids squeezed together tightly, wrinkling the skin at his temples, and he seemed to be talking to himself. ''Poor damn fool.''

Hilary was so angry she was afraid she'd cry. She balled her hands into fists and jammed them into her pockets again.

''Well,'' she told that strange, shadowed, unseeing face, ''if Marlene married Tommy for his money, where is it? Why does she have to beg you for baby clothes? Where's everything she inherited from her 'poor damn fool' of a husband?''

His eyes opened, and for a moment she thought she glimpsed the sparkle of dampness at their corners. But it must have been a trick of the light, for when he spoke his voice was tough and emotionless.

''She didn't inherit a thing, thank God. Tommy didn't have anything to leave her. My father left it all to me, and he told me to take care of Tommy. And do you want to know why?'' His voice grew harsh, daring her to ask.

"Why?"

"Because my father knew the world was full of people like your cousin. Gorgeous. Greedy. And ruthless enough to marry a man for his money, then spend the rest of her life making him miserable."

He might as well have slapped her. Her eyes stinging and blurring, she backed away from the desk, keeping her gaze fixed on Conner as if he held a weapon trained on her. Her only coherent thought was to get out of that room.

But at the door she stopped. "If that's the way you feel," she said, hating the way her voice shook, "why are you letting her stay here?"

He gave a low, ugly snort of laughter. "Isn't that obvious? Marlene's holding all the aces. She knows that, no matter how she behaves, I'm not letting that baby get away from me. That baby she carries may be, just may be, the only thing left of my brother."

"*May* be?" What was he implying? Suddenly dizzy, Hilary grasped for the door.

He nodded, rhythmically running his thumb around the rim of his glass. "Then again it may not be. It may merely be the joker in the deck." His voice had sunk, until again he seemed to be talking to himself. "We'll have to wait and see."

Hilary was incredulous. She squeezed the door between her fingers, hating him, hating his hideous, ridiculous implications and the weary indifference with which he voiced them. Oh, poor Marlene, who had been through so much and now found herself dependent on this . . . this heartless, unfeeling—

"Are you trying to make me believe," she said tightly, "that Marlene's baby is *not* your brother's child?"

He glanced up at her, seeming to just remember her presence. His eyelids drooped, as though holding them open required too much effort. "Are you so sure it is?"

"Of course I am!" She frowned at him. "She was crazy about Tommy. She was his *wife*. She..." Hilary was at a loss for words. How could you prove something that should be taken for granted? How could you explain that some things were impossible simply because they were unthinkable? "I'm sure," she finished, settling for the absolute, unqualified conviction she felt, "because I know Marlene."

He stared at her a long time before answering, so long that she began to get uneasy. His eyes were haunted, unfocused. He looked, suddenly, like a little boy who had awakened in the middle of an endless, unhappy night, confused and desperate for comfort.

The image startled her. She knew that look, all too well. She'd seen it often on Terri's face during the past year, while Terri struggled out of her deep depression. Why should this thirty-three-year-old businessman remind her of a brokenhearted nineteen-year-old?

But his eyes had drifted shut, locking the haunted expression into the privacy of his soul.

"You may be right," was all he said. "I hope you are. I hope to God you are."

WHEN HILARY FOUND her way down to the breakfast room the next morning, she was stunned to find Marlene there ahead of her. Marlene had always been a late sleeper, preferring the amusement of night to the drudgery of day, and Hilary had fully expected her to sleep until noon.

Hilary blinked to clear away the hallucination, then double-checked her watch. No, it hadn't stopped. Only nine o'clock, and Marlene was downstairs, fully dressed in a pink silk outfit that was as pale and sweet as cake frosting, her hair brushed to gleaming and caught at her neck in an oversize pink bow. She stood at the window, munching on a piece of toast and humming something tuneless but unmistakably merry.

"Will wonders never cease?" Hilary murmured, pouring herself a cup of coffee from the silver pot on the sideboard. She wandered over to the window and gave Marlene's ponytail a tweak. "Marlene meets the morning!"

Marlene's lips, satiny with a pink gloss that matched her outfit, opened in a wide smile. "Yeah, I know," she said sheepishly. "But it's such a beautiful morning, isn't it?"

Hilary made a skeptical noise. She wouldn't have thought it was Marlene's kind of day at all. During the night clouds had rolled in, driven by a tempestuous wind that had kept Hilary up half the night, going over and over the ugly scene in Conner's office until she thought she'd go crazy.

She'd finally slept a little, and when she awoke the wind had seemed much more subdued. But even now the air was alive with leaves that spiraled crazily before flinging themselves against the picture window, where they clung like flecks of red paint.

A beautiful morning? "Since when have you, the suntan queen, been a fan of rainy days?"

Marlene's smile broadened, and her blue eyes twinkled. "Since *this!*" Slipping one slim hand into the pocket of her dress, she pulled out a large rectangle of yellow paper. "This could brighten up even the gloomiest day."

Hilary set her untouched cup on the breakfast table and reached for the paper, which her cousin was waving triumphantly in front of her face. It was clearly a check. And it must be a generous one, to judge by Marlene's sparkling eyes.

"Hold still." Catching Marlene's wrist, Hilary brought the fluttering paper to a halt. Her eyes widened as she read the amount written there, followed by Conner St. George's bold, black signature. Generous. More than generous.

After what he'd said last night, this was the last thing Hilary had expected. She read the figure over and over, as if it was a code she couldn't decipher.

"So let it rain, I say." Marlene's voice was gay. "When you're inside the best stores in town having the time of your life, what does a little rain matter?" She pulled the check away and tucked it into her pocket, patting it satisfactorily.

"Well?" She nudged Hilary. "Let's go shopping!"

Hilary didn't move. "What did he say?" she asked slowly, still trying to make sense of it.

Her cousin paused by the door, examining her makeup in a mirror that hung over the sideboard. "What did who say?"

"Conner." Perching on the edge of the table, Hilary brushed at the tablecloth, trying to sound nonchalant. She didn't meet Marlene's eyes in the mirror. She didn't want Marlene to suspect how surprised she was. She certainly didn't want Marlene ever to guess what bitter, suspicious things Conner had said last night.

She took a sip of her coffee and looked up. "What did Conner say when he gave you the check?"

Marlene smoothed her forefinger over the curve of her upper lip, urging any stray lipstick back within bounds. "Nothing." Using her little finger, she feathered her brows into perfect arches. "I didn't see him at all. The check was on the table in the foyer when I woke up. Just the check and a note that said, 'for the baby.'"

For the baby. Hilary swallowed hard, trying to rid herself of the coffee's bitter aftertaste. He'd left this princely sum so Marlene could buy things for the baby. The baby that "just may be" all that was left of Tommy St. George.

The resentment that had been constricting Hilary's heart eased a little. This must be Conner's way of admitting that his accusations had been out of line. He hadn't meant it, not really. She should have known that he couldn't believe such horrible things. He'd been drinking, and he'd let his unhappiness override his better judgment.

Her eagerness to forgive him startled her. Maybe she felt lenient because he seemed so troubled. Even at her most furious, she'd known he wasn't just being spiteful. His unhappiness was real. And frighteningly powerful.

In fact, Hilary hadn't been able to stop thinking about the haunted look she'd glimpsed in his eyes. That look, more than the storm, had kept her up half the night, miserably stretching her emotions between fury and pity. Why was he so desperately unhappy? Was it just the loss of his brother—or was it something more? She felt an unreasonably intense desire to find out and then help him vanquish whatever dragons were plaguing him.

"Come on!" Marlene tugged impatiently at Hilary's sweater. "This check's burning a hole in my pocket."

With effort, Hilary shook herself loose from her disturbing thoughts. It wasn't her problem. Conner had made it quite clear that he found her presence a necessary inconvenience and would not welcome any intimacy.

But that didn't matter. Marlene was happy. Hilary had expected to spend the morning cheering up a despondent, self-pitying teenager. Instead, she found a smiling young woman, radiant in her pink-frosting maternity dress, looking exactly as an expectant mother should.

And that was Hilary's first—her *only*—mission here in the Smoky Mountains. Make Marlene happy.

Conner St. George could take care of his own dragons.

THE DISCUSSION HAD long since ceased to be produc-
tive.

Too tired to care anymore, Conner abandoned his
chair by the living-room fire and moved to the window, trying to escape the din created by one of his vice
presidents, Joe Bradley, and his lawyer, Gil Lunsford, who bickered behind him, loudly disagreeing on
everything, obviously unaware of his withdrawal.

He watched their reflections in the windowpane
with a curious detachment. They looked like a couple
of bantam roosters. And they were his top men, God
help him. He stifled a yawn. Were they always so tire-
somely pugnacious?

In fairness, he knew they weren't. He'd called the
men to his house and set this tempest in motion with
his own opening speech. He'd given them one hour to
come up with a plan to discover who had leaked information to the Dragon's Creek people, then to decide what could be done to save the deal. After a
moment of silence into which the panic was palpable,
they had erupted in this frantic gibberish.

Conner sighed, wondering suddenly what Hilary
and Marlene were doing. Were they still shopping? He
had expected them home by now. Maybe they were
lingering over dinner, sipping coffee, picking out
names and colleges for the baby. Marlene would love
that, and instinctively he knew that Hilary would in-
dulge her. She was like that—a born nurturer.

But it had gotten dark, and the mountain roads were tricky for a Floridian accustomed to flat terrain. He scanned the winding drive, looking for headlights.

As the volume behind him peaked, Conner checked his watch. Almost nine. The hour was up, and Gil and Joe didn't sound one iota closer to a plan. Joe was off on a tangent, lamenting the decline of corporate loyalty as if his armchair were a pulpit, and Gil was talking through him, drawing imaginary lines in the sand. "And that's our limit!" He shook a finger at his invisible adversary. "Not one penny higher!"

Groaning, Conner shut his eyes, which felt gritty and dry, as they always did these days. The dull throb in his temples had become a constant companion, too. He couldn't listen to much more of this. They sounded so stupid, like belligerent little boys quarreling over a baseball-card trade gone bad. *I wouldn't give you my Roger Clemens for fifty Nolan Ryans, you cheater!* Good God—he'd almost rather be choosing baby names.

His hand, which had been absently rubbing his mouth, froze. What was he saying? Must be sleep deprivation. He pressed the bridge of his nose, trying to ease the throbbing, trying to steady a world that seemed to be tilting. It *had* to be sleep deprivation. Business had never sounded stupid to him before, and wild horses couldn't have dragged him into a conversation about babies. He was starting to sound like Tommy.

Tommy. Sudden pain scratched like a thorn, and his throat closed convulsively. *Oh, Tommy, why couldn't I make things right for you?*

With a start he realized the room had grown quiet. His eyes flew open, and he spun around to see Gil and Joe rising to their feet, smiles replacing their worried scowls as they welcomed Hilary and Marlene home.

Gil jumped in first, coaxing the shopping bags from Marlene's hands. "Here, let me take these. You sit down."

Marlene smiled prettily, looking more relaxed than Conner had seen her in months. No doubt, thanks to Hilary, who had probably pampered her unstintingly all day. Only total indulgence could bring a smile like that to Marlene's lips. Or a good flirt. Conner watched cynically as Gil urged Marlene into the armchair, his chivalry providing the perfect topping for her day, like the cherry on a hot fudge sundae.

"Mmm, that feels fantastic." Marlene leaned back in the chair and extended her legs, wiggling her feet. "We really did shop till we dropped, huh, Hilary? My feet are killing me!"

The sight of Gil's eyes, about to pop as he watched the slim ankles rotate, gave Conner his first chuckle of the day. Gil, only in his late twenties, bald and having a vicious mid-life crisis, was a sucker for this long-legged woman-child.

Joe, on the other hand, couldn't take his eyes off Hilary, who was busily stacking bags and boxes in the corner. With exaggerated, surreptitious hand gestures, he tried to get Conner to come over and introduce them, something Conner was strangely loathe to do. Joe was a married man, for God's sake. Peg, Joe's wife and the mother of his three children, certainly wouldn't like the look in her husband's eyes right now.

Not that Conner could blame him, for he was looking, too. It must be misty out, he thought irrelevantly. Hilary's long, auburn hair was damp and clung with an unconscious sensuality to her forehead and cheeks before spilling down her back. And she was wearing a sweater so soft the urge to touch it was damn near irresistible. It was red and green and yellow and orange, all kinds of colors woven into patterns that might have been leaves, or flowers, or nothing at all, but it made her eyes so amazingly green....

Conner's body tightened in a response that was becoming embarrassingly familiar. He fought it down, using anger as a club. What was happening to him? Last night she'd been Juliet. Today she was some kind of wood nymph. Of all the adolescent, slack-jawed...

Get a grip, he told himself angrily. One mid-life crisis in the room was enough.

But she was smiling at him, joining him in his corner of the room, much to the apparent disgust of Joe, who found himself stuck with the cooing Gil and Marlene.

"It was nice of you to give Marlene such a generous check," Hilary said, putting her hand on Conner's arm, and he had to start the fight with his body all over again. "Why don't we just pretend last night never happened? Truce?"

Conner didn't know what to say. Hilary clearly assumed the gesture meant he'd thought better of the things he'd said. But it didn't mean that at all. His suspicions were as strong as ever.

No, his motive for leaving the check was much simpler. He'd done it because he wanted to see Hilary Fairfax smile. At him.

And now that she had, he didn't want her to stop. Not yet. "Truce," he lied and put his hand over hers.

CHAPTER FIVE

IT WAS A COLD, quiet 3 A.M., and Hilary paused in the dark hall, trying to identify the strange sound she'd just heard. Her heart beat steadily but rapidly against her breastbone. She'd been so sure she was the only person awake, and then, startlingly, the sound had echoed into the silence. Not quite a word and not quite a cry, but definitively human and full of emotion. Swollen, somehow, with pain.

It had not been a television, she decided, or any kind of electronic babble, because no other noises followed. The house was eerily quiet, as though even the bricks and wood and glass were asleep.

She glanced down the hall, trying to get her bearings, then frowned, reaching an uncomfortable conclusion. Unless she had completely turned herself around during this nocturnal expedition, she was now only a couple of feet away from Conner's suite.

Yes, those must be his rooms, where a wing jutted off to one side. That right-hand door was to his office. The door on the left must be to the games room, where last night she'd glimpsed a billiard table. Her gaze ran along the wall and halted at the middle door, the only door that had been firmly shut last night. His bedroom door.

Suddenly a rustling whisper slithered through the air, and Hilary held her breath, listening. It came again quickly, emanating like invisible smoke from under Conner's bedroom door. And then again. And again, until finally she recognized it. The sound of someone shifting restlessly on expensive sheets.

Without thinking, she moved toward the door. Was he ill? Had he been calling for help? Perhaps she could...

One hand was on the doorknob, the other poised and ready to knock, before she came to her senses. She froze there, horrified at what she'd been about to do, paralyzed by a piercing mental image of Conner's masculine body tangled in the sheets.

What on earth would he think if she knocked on his door at three in the morning? She tried to imagine him rising, coming to the door, those blue-gray eyes heavy with sleep, that body clad in—or *not* clad in...

She flushed, a scalp-to-toe, swamping heat. Her velour robe trapped the warmth, holding it against her skin until she felt sauna-damp with embarrassment and nerves. She had to get out of here.

"No! *Wait!*"

Conner's voice roared out, smashing the silence. Her heart catapulting into her throat, Hilary jumped away from the door. She propped herself against the wall, heart pounding, as his fierce words reverberated through the empty corridor.

She breathed through her mouth, watching the blank door, half-expecting it to open. Who was he talking to?

"The key." Conner's voice was softer this time, but more desperate. The thrashing sounds began again, and Hilary stared. What was happening in there?

"For God's sake, the key!"

And then a groan, a long, descending moan of helplessness that seemed to pull her heart down along with it. "No," he mumbled, his voice no longer clear, as if he had turned his face to the pillow. "No, no, no, no..."

Hilary shut her eyes. No one, especially not a stranger, should witness such unguarded misery. And for a man like Conner, a proud, willful man accustomed to control and despising those who lacked it...

Instinctively she knew he would never forgive her for hearing this.

"Please." He was begging now, and her heart twisted. "Please, no."

As though conjured up by the pain in his voice, a tear ran down her cheek. She couldn't stand it. If she stayed, she would have to fling away the barrier of the door and hold him until the nightmare was gone. And then...

She swallowed, sobered by the thought. And then...what?

Then they would just be two strangers again. When the crisis passed and they found themselves clutched in a moonlight intimacy, they'd both feel like fools. And he would hate her for what she knew.

She couldn't do it. Before he could utter another heartbreaking word, a word that might make her do something she'd regret, she gathered the hem of her robe in her fists and fled.

Dreams of doors without keys and dragons drowning in the rain troubled her all night, but much to her surprise, she slept late and awoke to a bright, blue morning.

She raised her window, hoping to clear her muddy head. It was one of those perfect autumn days. Not a single cloud remained from yesterday's iron-gray sky, but she knew that today's glory was possible only because of yesterday's storms. The wind had shaken any dull, brown leaves from the branches, and the deluge of rain had washed all the dirt from the air. Only purified beauty remained. The ice-crystal sound of the brook carried all the way to her room, and the forest looked as if it had been decorated for a party, the trees hung with streamers of russet and plum, topaz and gold.

Yes, the world had endured the storm, and the rewards were great. Maybe, she thought as she lowered the window reluctantly, that was a lesson she could take into her own day.

She pulled on jeans and a turtleneck and tried to be optimistic, though her head pounded miserably and she dreaded encountering Conner. She shuddered to think what his haunted sleep might have done to his already-frayed temper. Unfortunately she doubted he was the type to wax philosophical about the calm after the storm.

Sure enough, when she ventured downstairs, both Marlene and Conner were seated in the breakfast alcove, nearly empty plates in front of them and the air thick with tension and the slightly burned aroma of coffee brewed too long.

Hilary knew instantly that something was wrong. Marlene looked adorable in a dress as yellow as the sunshine, but her face was a sullen pout and she picked at the remains of her toast, casting sulky sidelong glances at Conner every few seconds. Conner, in marked contrast, was reading the paper with sublime indifference to Marlene's theatrics.

Although Hilary said good-morning with a determined smile, she groaned inwardly. Good God, what now?

"Hilary," Marlene started in immediately, her voice high and grieved, the tone of a child tattling, "Conner won't take me to my appointment with the obstetrician this morning."

Hilary flashed a look at Conner. He returned the gaze calmly. "I can't. I have to go to Dallas."

Marlene swung her foot angrily and tapped her knife against her plate. "See? He knew I had a doctor's appointment today."

"I also knew that Hilary could take you." He had gone back to the newspaper and spoke without looking up.

"But *you've* always taken me to my appointments, Conner." Marlene rested her hand on Conner's sleeve, her fingers slim and pink-tipped against the soft wool of his gray jacket. "Always."

"Because there was no one else to do it." Conner lifted Marlene's hand and put it on the table. Almost as an afterthought, as though he didn't want to seem cruel, he added, "Hilary's here now. She can take you."

"Of course I'll take you." Hilary put as much enthusiasm as she could into the offer. "It'll be fun. You can show me the rest of the town. We saw only baby boutiques yesterday."

The last was a rather unsubtle reminder of yesterday's manic shopping trip. Only twenty-four hours ago, as they careened from baby store to baby store, Marlene had gushingly worshiped the generous Conner and his bottomless checking account.

But Marlene wasn't ready to be placated. She crossed her arms over the mound of her stomach and turned her head away, staring haughtily at the wall.

It was a ridiculous display of adolescent temper, and Hilary had a very un-cousinly urge to shake her. Marlene obviously craved Conner's attention and time, and although Hilary could sympathize with Marlene's loneliness, she cringed to see the younger girl acting so bratty.

Did she really think this was the way to interest a man like Conner? Hilary could feel his disgust as he crisply folded the newspaper and got to his feet, preparing to make his escape. Why couldn't Marlene feel it, too?

"Conner," Marlene whined in a last-ditch effort to stop him, "what if something's gone wrong?" She rubbed her hands down her stomach anxiously, as though she suspected something was going wrong at that very moment. Her voice was weak; she sounded

charmingly pathetic. Hilary's urge to shake her inten-
sified.

"Like what?" Conner was skeptical, his eyes hard
as he followed the movement of Marlene's hands up
the rounded yellow silk and down again, hesitating
once when the baby kicked, jostling the silk quite vis-
ibly in an uncooperative show of robust health.

"Like—" Marlene bit her lower lip "—like I've had
some pains. I'm scared, Conner. Dr. Pritchard said
that was a bad sign. What if I go into labor or something? It's too soon."

Hilary was fascinated by the play of emotions across
Conner's face. His first reaction was annoyed incre-
dulity, scorn flattening his wide mouth into a grim
line. He knew he was being manipulated, and he didn't
like it. Hilary waited for the scathing words to come
out, blasting Marlene and her tricks into their place.

But just as clearly, Hilary saw the moment doubt set
in. Conner's eyes darkened, the gray abruptly smothering the blue, and though he was still angry, it became the frustrated anger of a man who has stepped
into a hidden but inescapable trap. His common sense
told him to dismiss Marlene's whining, but anxiety
had clamped steel teeth into him, and he couldn't
wrench loose.

For the first time Hilary fully understood what
Conner had told her in his office. Marlene, he had said
bitterly, is holding all the aces.

It was so true, Hilary saw now, so dangerously true.
For a sad teenage widow, Marlene played her cards
amazingly well. And she certainly knew the value of

an ace. Whether Conner admitted it or not, this baby was important to him. The very suggestion that his brother's child might be in jeopardy had turned his face to ash, his resistance to dust. Hilary knew before he spoke that he would capitulate. He would do anything for this baby. Anything.

And suddenly the whole situation took on frightening new proportions. Hilary looked from Conner to Marlene and back again, her pulse racing uncomfortably. What could possibly come of a situation like this? Eventually the baby would be born—a baby that was not Conner's own child, no matter how much he loved it. Marlene was his sister-in-law, not his wife....

Hilary's breath, which had been coming quickly, suddenly stopped. How far, exactly, would Conner go for this baby? How far would Marlene *make* him go? All the way to the altar?

No! Hilary couldn't imagine a better recipe for disaster than the marriage of these two completely unsuited people who had neither love nor respect, neither friendship nor passion, between them.

"So will you please go with me?" Marlene knew she had won. Hilary could see it in her eyes. She was happy again; she had gotten her way. "Please? You do see that I need you. You do see, don't you?"

Conner nodded. "I do," he said, and the words made Hilary shiver.

MARLENE'S SMUG TRIUMPH didn't last long. The minute they arrived home Conner disappeared. Business calls, he explained tersely, heading for his office.

Hilary, watching him, saw the disdain for Marlene that warred with his concern for the baby and thought perhaps her cousin would come to regret this particularly petty victory. For two whole hours Conner had been Marlene's captive, but he was a dangerous prisoner, contemptuous and completely untamed.

Marlene, who obviously missed all those nuances, pouted and headed straight for bed, complaining of a headache.

Relieved to be left alone, Hilary curled up on the sofa with a book open in her lap. She didn't read much, her mind wrestling with all the complications she'd glimpsed this morning. She'd known the situation was tricky, but this... This was a lot like standing on a tightrope, she thought, and discovering there was quicksand beneath.

Suddenly she wanted to talk to Terri. Yes, that's what was wrong with her. She was homesick, missing her sister. Dropping her book, she hurried into the sunny kitchen and plopped down at the built-in desk, pulling the telephone toward her.

But the girl who answered the dorm phone said Terri wouldn't be back until much later. She had classes and was going to a party after that. If it was really important, the girl said, Hilary could try calling the party tonight. She offered the phone number.

Though she knew she probably wouldn't call Terri there—she wouldn't want to look as if she were checking up on her—Hilary asked for the number just in case. But she hadn't brought a pen with her. She scouted around the desktop, but nothing came to hand. Then she tried the drawers. String, scissors, paper clips—the usual kitchen hodgepodge. But no pencils.

"Hold on just a minute." Frustrated, she pulled open another drawer, and this time she hit the jackpot. At least three dozen pens and pencils, two crayons, an eyebrow pencil...

But there was something else, something that didn't belong here. A small, black velvet box. A jeweler's box.

"You find a pencil?" The girl was getting impatient.

"What?" Hilary had almost forgotten that the coed was there. She was turning the little box over in her hand, wondering whether it would be a disgraceful breach of etiquette to open it. "Oh, yes. Go ahead."

But she never even heard the number. Her fingers had a will of their own and no manners at all. They flipped open the box—and then almost dropped it. Inside, propped on white satin, was the loveliest diamond ring she had ever seen.

Three carats...maybe more? She had no experience judging these things. She knew only that it was very big but not a bit vulgar. So beautiful. It caught the sunshine, trapping it in its cool depths, then throwing it out again in winking flashes of blue and red and brilliant white.

Trying to sound normal, Hilary thanked the girl and hung up. For a long time she sat numbly in the chair and stared at the diamond. What was something like this doing shoved into a kitchen drawer like a piece of junk? Whose was it?

But of course it was Conner's. It had to be. The real question was—who did he buy it for? She suddenly felt light-headed and slightly sick, as the most obvious possibility leapt to mind. No, she said out loud to the empty kitchen and snapped the box shut. Not Marlene. He wouldn't do it.

Not even for the baby? No. She wouldn't believe it. She had seen how he looked at Marlene. The only emotion her cousin elicited from Conner St. George was disdain.

Then who? But it was none of her business. Hilary thrust the box back into the drawer, feeling a little like Pandora.

"Sorry. I didn't know you were making a call."

Conner had entered the kitchen behind her. How long ago? How much had he seen? She glanced up guiltily, her face reddening as if she'd been caught stealing the damn diamond, not just looking at it.

"I'm finished," she said awkwardly, gesturing at the cradled receiver. "She was out." Conner was wearing the bottom half of a steel-blue jogging suit. He must have just taken off the top, because he rubbed his face with it before tossing it onto the kitchen counter as he went by. His hair was damp at the nape, and his entire torso had a glistening sheen, as if he'd been running hard.

Hadn't he said he had to make business calls? Obviously that had been an excuse, an exit line. He must have slipped out his office door and taken a run through the woods. Hilary found the thought strangely reassuring. You didn't marry a woman you were already running away from.

"Were you calling your sister?" Opening the refrigerator, he twisted the cap from a bottle of spring water, which he polished off in one long swig.

"Yes," Hilary said, watching the perspiration trickle down the muscular column of his throat, down into the dark hair of his tanned chest, as he drank. How did he manage to look so sexy when he was working out? When she was sweating she just looked...sweaty. "I wanted to see if she's okay. But she's out all day—classes and a party, and—"

She wrenched the faucet of words shut. Why was she telling him all this? It had just been a polite question. He didn't really care. But he looked so damnably masculine, half-dressed in those trousers that were loose-fitting and yet made of a fabric so soft they fit him like a second skin. With his chest bare, he seemed all shoulders. As he reached over to dump the bottle in the recycling bin, the muscles of his back rippled and expanded. And again those pants! They outlined the trim, hard curve of his rear as if they had been custom-tailored.

Blinking violently, Hilary turned her head away, shocked. What had gotten into her? She wasn't the kind of woman who sat around staring at men's rears! How many times had she chided Marlene and Terri for just this sort of nonsense? Hundreds. "It's the other end that counts, girls," she'd teased until she could say it in her sleep. And she'd meant it. Hard, beautiful bodies too often came attached to hard, ugly egos.

"Well, if Terri's that busy, then she must be doing fine." Conner turned around and gave Hilary his best, dimpling smile.

Hilary nodded. "Sounds that way." She needed to get hold of herself. It wasn't as if she'd never seen a bare male chest before. Where was her infamous immunity, the pride of the Fairfax women?

But he wasn't finished testing that immunity yet.

"Can I get you anything?" he asked. When she shook her head, he dropped with casual grace onto the chair next to her. Leaning back, he hitched his trousers up slightly to accommodate his muscular thighs and settled in, spreading his legs comfortably and hooking his fingertips in his pockets.

The position was utterly masculine, disturbingly sexy, though she sensed he hadn't meant it to be so. He wasn't *trying* to make her heart race—but it raced anyway. Men like that were the most dangerous of all. They never *tried* to break your heart, but they'd shattered it, anyway.

Now that he was so close, she could smell his wetness—a delicious dampness, as clean and healthy as rain, or the brook that ran outside her window. Her lungs asked for more of the smell, and she found herself inhaling deeply.

Damn. Looking away, she toyed with the pencil, doodling on the scrap of notepaper in front of her. What was going on here?

Maybe, she thought with an attempt at rationality, maybe she was overly sensitized to him because of last night, when they'd been only a door apart, neither of them able to sleep. How strange that he didn't know she'd been there. She'd been intensely aware of him, emotionally affected by what he'd endured.

She slanted a look at him. How long had those nightmares been going on? How often did he have them? And more importantly, what were they about?

But the questions would have to go unanswered. She could never ask him. Even now, half-naked and beaded with perspiration, he managed to look autocratic and unapproachable.

He was a lot like her father, she recognized with a sudden chill. They both had a natural arrogance that repelled unwelcome prying. Which, of course, was why it had taken her mother ten years to find out about the affairs....

"Why don't you invite her up for the weekend?"

Hilary had to concentrate to remember what they had been talking about. Oh, yes. Terri. "Up here?"

One corner of his mouth pulled up, tucking into the dimple. "Well, this *is* where you are."

The lopsided smile was so contagious that Hilary found herself smiling, too. He seemed sincere. And the suggestion was tempting.

A trill of happiness skipped through her. It would be heavenly to see Terri. If they could spend a couple of days together, she'd know for sure that her little sister was all right.

"It's a lovely offer," she said, trying not to gush. "But I'd hate to take advantage of your hospitality. I know you have a lot of work to do, and you won't want a house full of females."

He shook his head, rubbing his neck. "I may not even be here this weekend. I leave for Dallas in a couple of hours. I don't know when I'll be back. Not for at least a week."

She was surprised and, though she didn't fully understand why, a little disappointed. Perhaps it was just that she'd have to spend the entire time consoling Marlene, who would, of course, be devastated.

"Why? What's in Dallas?"

"Just outside Dallas, actually. A dude ranch for sale that could be turned into a nice little resort. It's a good deal. It's making money—more than Dragon's Creek has made in years."

She frowned, stunned by his nonchalant tone. "Does this mean you're abandoning Dragon's Creek Resort?" She couldn't believe it. She knew he wanted Dragon's Creek, wanted it so badly it hurt. She could feel it every time he so much as said the words. She had heard that same sharp hunger in her father's voice so often. "You really might buy a dude ranch, instead?"

He grinned rakishly, lifting both brows in feigned innocence. "Not in a million years."

"But..." Had lack of sleep affected her brain? She was lost.

"But the Dragon's Creek people are going to *think* I might."

"Oh." She felt indescribably dense. Hadn't she learned anything from the years with her father? Business, business, business. Lies, lies, lies. "It's all for show, then? The trip to Dallas, the dude ranch..."

"I'll look at the place," he said indifferently. "But, yes, it's pretty much all for show. It's like a dance, you see. In, out, forward, back—"

"Do-si-do and allemande left?"

"Exactly." He smiled again.

"You think this is fun." Her comment was not a question. Her father had thought the same thing. Deals, negotiations, bluffs, manipulation—these had been the ruling passions of his life. Business was absolutely paramount. She had known her father to fire an employee for speaking disloyally about his company. A bitter irony, really, coming from the man who had cheated on his wife with three secretaries and discarded his whole family for number four.

"It's fun if I win." Conner wasn't smiling anymore. Apparently this was too serious to joke about. "It's important to be the choreographer in this dance. Much less fun, I'd think, to have someone else calling the steps."

"What if they don't fall for it?"

"Then I'll try something else." His voice had an edge to it, and for a moment Hilary pitied the Dragon's Creek people. "I'm going to have that resort. My father created Dragon's Creek. It was the cornerstone of our company."

"So why did you sell it?"

"We didn't." Conner's voice was bleak, and he stood up, as though the conversation made him too restless to sit. "My uncle did. When my father got sick, I was still in school, not ready, really, to run the company. My uncle seemed like the logical choice to take over until either I was old enough or my father was strong enough to step back in."

He scooped up his sweatshirt and wadded it into a ball. "The only hitch was that my uncle was an artist, not a businessman."

"Really? Tommy was an artist, too, wasn't he?" Hilary knew the minute she said the words that they were a mistake. She had hoped to distract Conner from this unpleasant recitation, but the mention of Tommy seemed only to darken his mood further.

"Yes. And that's why my father left everything to me. Tommy and my uncle were alike—neither one of them had a grain of business sense. My uncle only had control of the company for a couple of years, but he nearly destroyed it. He had such grand ideas, overexpanding in a down economy, overpaying for bad properties, mortgaging the good ones until he was drowning in debt. Before I got out of graduate school he had lost all the bigger resorts, including Dragon's Creek."

He tossed the sweatshirt onto the table with so much force that it slid all the way across and ended up on the floor. "The whole fiasco killed my father."

Hilary shook her head, not disputing his claim, but trying somehow to ward off the anger she felt radiating from him. "I'm sorry," she said meaninglessly.

He met her sympathy with a glare. "Don't be. All that doesn't matter anymore. What's important is that by this time next week, I'll have the Dragon back."

His father's death didn't matter? Sickened, Hilary rose to her feet. She didn't want to hear any more. And to think just moments ago she was admiring this man's beauty!

Her immunity had returned, full force. She knew all about men like Conner St. George. Why had she ever worried that Marlene might be able to maneuver him into marriage? Instead, she should have worried that Conner might maneuver Marlene out of her rights to her own child. Marlene, for all her devious tricks, was an infant compared to Conner. She was just another dancer, a bit part, really. He'd never allow her to get in his way.

But what if the baby took after Tommy? What if he was born with the fatal weakness—an artistic temperament and no business sense? Then Marlene's maternal rights would be safe enough. After all, what happened to dancers who weren't able to kick high enough, twirl fast enough? They were cut from the show, weren't they? Replaced with other dancers who had more talent.

And remembering the way he'd gotten her up to the mountains for his convenience, she had the infuriating feeling that she, too, had become an official member of his chorus line.

To hell with him. "I need to check on Marlene," she said briskly, dropping her pencil onto the desk. *And get away from you.*

"I'll come with you. I need to call Dr. Pritchard."

His tone implied that Dr. Pritchard would be sitting around awaiting just such a call. So Dr. Pritchard, too, was part of the company, Hilary thought bitterly as she exited the kitchen. He'd be eager to promise Conner anything.

But could he? Could he really promise Conner the things he wanted? Could he promise that Marlene and the baby would be fine? No. Conner was not calling the tune on this one. No one, not Dr. Pritchard, not even Conner St. George, could tell Marlene's baby what to do—whether to be a girl or a boy, smart or dumb, business-minded or artistic. He couldn't even tell it when to be born.

Good for you, Baby. Hilary's spirits lifted, thinking of that little being, the one person in this whole drama who didn't know what Conner St. George wanted and didn't give a damn.

CHAPTER SIX

IT WAS NINETY DEGREES in the dusty flatlands of Culpepper, Texas, and Conner couldn't stand the place another minute. Halfway through the tour, he found it impossible to pretend he'd even consider buying this dude ranch from hell. Five hundred acres of tumbleweed and dirt, where sweating, swaybacked horses plodded along with overweight tourists on their backs. Buy it? You couldn't *give* it to him! He was leaving.

When he told them over breakfast, Gil and Tom were horrified. He'd spoil everything, they said. It was only Sunday; the Dragon's Creek people would know the ranch deal was a bluff and wouldn't bring down the price so much as a penny.

But Conner didn't care. And when he said those three blasphemous words, Gil was silent, his egg-laden fork frozen on its way to his mouth, shock written all over his face. So Conner said them again. "I don't care."

He threw his clothes into his suitcase and hopped on the next flight to North Carolina, leaving Gil to apologize to the ranch brokers. He wanted to breathe crisp mountain air. He wanted to see the red-and-yellow mountains roll off endlessly into the mist. He wanted to go home.

And for once in his connect-the-dots life he was going to do what he wanted. He didn't care if it meant paying top dollar, or three times top dollar, for Dragon's Creek. He was tired of playing charades, tired of shadowboxing, tired of...well, he was just plain tired.

The jet streaked through the blue Texas sky like a rocket, but still seemed too slow, and Conner's nerves jangled with impatience. He felt an obscure dread that he would be too late, though he had no idea what he'd be too late for.

It was only two o'clock Sunday afternoon when he let himself into the house, but utter, midnight silence greeted him.

"Hello?" He put his suitcase down in the foyer, the sound echoing mockingly. "Anybody home?"

No one answered. They were gone. He was too late, after all. He scanned the empty hall, surprised by the intensity of his disappointment. He hadn't realized how much he hated an empty house.

Thinking perhaps a scotch would keep him company, he moved to the bar and poured himself a shot. He was staring at the drink, hating the sight and smell of it, when behind him he heard a flutelike trill of laughter, as sweet as the sound of a wood thrush. Holding the shot glass, he went to the picture window and looked down. At first he didn't see anything, though the laughter still hung on the air, playful now, like the dance of falling leaves. Where was it coming from?

And then he saw them—Hilary and her sister in the branches of a big oak tree. Terri was climbing, her back to him, but Hilary had found the perfect perch and was leaning against the massive trunk, her long legs stretched before her on the limb.

He almost dropped his drink. Good God, she was gorgeous. She was laughing, throwing her head back and looking so—"Healthy" seemed like such a stupid word, but it fit. She looked healthy, both physically and emotionally. He put his hand on the window, as if he could borrow some of that glowing health. But the window was cold, unyielding, not at all like touching her would be, and he let his hand fall.

In a moment, Marlene came wandering out of the shadow of the woods, small golden-leaved twigs tucked under her arm. Her smile was so unaffected that for a moment Conner couldn't see the petulant Lolita he was accustomed to living with.

Was that really Marlene? He had forgotten how young nineteen could be—for Pete's sake, she was practically a child! And yet, full with pregnancy, she couldn't climb the tree with the others, couldn't really *be* a child. It suddenly struck him as pitiful—that little girl with her swollen stomach, already a widow, about to be thrust into motherhood.

A sense of failure wriggled uncomfortably to life inside him. Perhaps, resenting her as he did, he had not been kind enough. She was infuriating, unbelievably spoiled and immature, querulous and demanding, but . . . he should have been kinder.

After all, she had lost Tommy, too. Perhaps he had been so exhausted from carrying his own burden of loss and guilt that he hadn't seen how heavy her burden was.

Yes, he should have been kinder. And he would be. He would be.

Spying Marlene, Hilary smiled and called out, swinging her legs down so that she straddled the branch. Her hair, which was as russet as the leaves over her head, blew in the light wind, glistening where the sun picked through the trees. She laughed again as she leaned forward, hugging the branch, and his gut twisted. He could remember when he, too, used to feel that way, fit, vigorous and stimulated by life.

Sliding the untouched shot glass onto the bar, he headed for the front door. It was not a conscious decision; he was drawn toward the three women like mindless metal to a magnet.

But again he was too late. By the time he made his way around, they were heading back to the house. They walked slowly, Hilary in the front, the other two straggling behind. Casually elegant in tight-fitting blue jeans, Hilary had pulled a gray cashmere jacket over her yellow sweater, and her tousled auburn hair was crowned with a circlet of the golden sassafras leaves Marlene had picked.

"Hi," he called, and all three women looked up, dumb with astonishment. He had said he'd be gone for a week; they clearly hadn't dreamed he'd return so soon. Hilary dragged the crown from her head and thrust it behind her back guiltily, as though she'd been caught playing hooky by the meanest teacher at school.

Conner frowned. Was that how she saw him? Irrationally the thought stung, and he wanted to reach inside her mind and rub out the unflattering image.

But, of course, he couldn't. Of all the women he'd ever known, Hilary Fairfax had the most inviolable control over her own thoughts. You could almost see the signs: No Trespassing.

But the man who'd just broken every rule in the business book didn't feel like obeying the signs today. So he reached around her waist, his arm pressing into the soft wool of her jacket, and pried the crown from her fingers.

She had no time to protest as he placed it carefully atop her head. Her hair was like silk, and his hands lingered, brushing back the strands that had fallen into her face. When his fingers touched her skin she stiffened. More signs, bigger and bolder: Keep Off.

"Wear it," he said, touching her cheek one more time while he marveled at his own stubborn disobedience. What had gotten into him today? "It looks good."

Good? What an understatement. She belonged here, he thought fiercely, forcing his hands into his pockets so that he could control them. She belonged in the woods, in the autumn, with leaves tangled in her hair and sun dappling her face. Her eyes were as green as summer's last few leaves, and where his fingers had smoothed her cheek she was flushing, her skin as rosy as wild cherries.

And suddenly he knew what was wrong with him. He wanted her. Wanted her painfully. What would she do, he wondered as he watched the color spread across her cheeks, if in this lawless mood he swept her up and carried her deep into the forest, so deep the others would never find them? Would she be furious? Or would she give in to some untapped primal urges of her own and simply wrap her arms around his neck and rest that silken head against his chest? Would she let him lay her on a quilt of leaves and make love to her until they—

Good God! With a desperate mental lunge he grabbed the reins of his galloping fantasies, yanking them to a stop. Was he positively insane? Carry her off? Make love to her? To borrow an expression he had used as a boy—you and whose army? Judging from the expression on her face right now, if he dared to so much as shake her hand she'd slap him senseless.

Just look at her. While he had been indulging in that brainless fit of pubescent prurience, she'd been withdrawing from him. Oh, she hadn't moved an inch, but her face had closed up, the light dying in her eyes, the smile fading from her mouth. She had become, in an instant, merely the statue of a woman, beautiful but remote, feeling nothing, revealing nothing, and most definitely offering nothing.

Why, damn it? He almost spoke the words out loud. *Why?*

Why was she so guarded, so unreachable? It was horribly frustrating, like grabbing for a reflection in the water only to have it dissolve and ripple away the minute you touched it.

Something tugged at his arm.

"Oh, Conner," Marlene exclaimed effusively from a spot near his shoulder, "I'm so glad you came back early!"

He looked down, temporarily bewildered. Had she been there this whole time? Amazing. He had forgotten the other women completely. Terri hung back shyly, half-hidden behind her sister, but while he'd been daydreaming, Marlene had attached herself to his arm like a leech.

Wonderful. He locked his muscles, trying to control the urge to heartlessly brush her off. Just wonderful. Was it some new law of irony that the women you desired turned to stone while the women you didn't want crawled all over you?

But in the nick of time he remembered his promise to himself. He wouldn't take out his frustrations on Marlene. He would be kinder, more patient, no matter how hard it was. And it was going to be *very* hard.

Somehow he managed to smile down at her.

"I've only been gone a few days," he said. "And you look like you've been having a grand time without me." He transferred the smile to Hilary, to let her know he gave her all the credit, but only the statue smiled back. She didn't care about the credit, the smile said. She didn't care *what* he thought.

Suddenly he was angry. How different that cold face was from the one he'd glimpsed from the window! It was unfair. *She* was unfair. He hadn't done anything terrible to her. He wanted to grab her by those cashmere lapels and demand an explanation, if necessary shaking her until the leaves fell from her hair.

"Oh, we've been having a ball," Marlene agreed blithely. "And we're going to the Dragon's Creek Art Festival this afternoon. It should be great fun. Want to come with us?"

Hilary moved, just a slight shift that he wouldn't have noticed if he hadn't been watching for it. It was an instinctive twitch of rejection. She didn't want to spend the afternoon with him.

Well, too bad. Though he hadn't for one minute considered tramping around the Arts Festival today—had, in fact, called a vice presidents' meeting for this afternoon—suddenly he wouldn't miss it for the world. Maybe during the long, chilly afternoon, he'd find a chance to chip away at Hilary's marble facade. Or if that failed, maybe he'd just grab her by the lapels and . . .

And see what happened.

IT WAS JUST as Hilary had feared. Before they'd been at the festival half an hour, Marlene and Terri had run off together, leaving her alone with Conner. Marlene had stayed as long as she could stand it, doggedly flirting with an unresponsive Conner, but finally, because she really was just a kid, the lure of cotton candy and girlish giggling was too great.

"She seems happy."

Hilary glanced at Conner, checking for signs of sarcasm, but amazingly finding none. He was staring after the disappearing pair, his lips actually curved into something like a smile.

Come to think of it, he had been unusually patient with Marlene all afternoon. Hilary couldn't help wondering why. She glanced again, surreptitiously, but the smile was still there. Why? The tinny sound of a banjo could be heard in the distance, and Hilary smelled deep-fried onion rings somewhere closer. This place was hardly a businessman's dream. Wasting time at an arts festival seemed quite out of character for Conner.

"Being with your sister seems good for her," he said as they strolled past rows of jam jars and pinecone door wreaths. "They're like a couple of kids."

Hilary nodded, suddenly aware that she had neglected her manners. "It's good for Terri, too. Thanks for letting me invite her to visit."

Conner brushed the formalities away. "How's Terri doing? Settling in at college okay?"

"Great." It was true, thank goodness. Terri really seemed to be herself for the first time in two frightening years. She'd been told that the creep's divorce was final, his ex-wife awarded every penny she'd asked for and more. The judgment had seemed to put the entire affair safely to rest, and Terri was ready to forget it and move on. She loved college, which seemed to be chock-full of darling, young, *unmarried* men.

"She's much better," Hilary went on. "In fact, she loves school so much she's trying to talk Marlene into taking a couple of classes after the baby's born."

Conner's pace slowed fractionally, and for a minute he didn't answer, concentrating on a row of handmade teddy bears. "College. That would be pretty difficult, I'd think," he said without looking at her. His voice was almost expressionless. "With a newborn to consider."

Almost expressionless, but not quite. Hilary heard the disapproval beneath the careful modulation, saw the tension in his strong, tanned fingers as they picked up a helpless bear. He didn't want Marlene to go to college. He didn't want Marlene to go anywhere.

Hilary took a quick breath. Oh, no. Was that what had brought on his atypical display of tolerance toward his sister-in-law? Could it be that Conner had decided he must be nice if he wanted Marlene to stay? If he wanted to marry her?

Quickly, though, his tension seemed to ease, and putting the bear down, he moved on to the next booth. With effort, Hilary followed. She must be imagining things. Conner was fourteen years older than Marlene, and more importantly, he could barely stand to be in the same room with her for five minutes. Surely the idea of marriage had never crossed his mind. Or even if it had, surely he was too sensible to entertain it for long.

But it definitely had crossed Marlene's mind. This weekend had been an extended slumber party for Marlene and Terri, and Hilary, as a sort of chaperon, had heard things. She had heard the girls making those wild plans that only teenage girls alone at midnight can make. Oh, yes, Lord help them all, the idea had crossed Marlene's mind. Hilary had spent all weekend trying to think what she should do.

"But there's plenty of time to decide all that later, isn't there?" Conner's voice was firm but upbeat. "Let's look around, shall we? Did you know that this land will be part of the deal when we buy Dragon's Creek?"

"No." Hilary felt herself stumbling in the conversational dance, as if someone had changed tempo midsong. She had been mentally girding herself for a confrontation—who should decide what was best for Marlene's future, anyway? But this Conner, this affable, easygoing man, was a stranger to her. He apparently had no interest in a confrontation.

"So, where to next?" Without waiting for an answer, he puckered his lips and whistled a few notes of the bluegrass ditty that wafted toward them. He ambled over to a stall where three old men sat whittling pieces of wood into amazingly lifelike dolls.

Hilary hung back, still feeling caught wrong-footed. It was as if there was nothing in the world he'd rather do than this. As if he no longer needed to hold meetings day and night to plot the takeover of Dragon's Creek.

Well, of course—she stopped in her tracks—how could she have been so obtuse? That must be it: his trip to Texas had been a success. He looked— Well, happy wasn't exactly the right word, but he definitely looked different, like a man who'd been released from some intangible constraint. Liberated.

"Look at the workmanship in these." He held up a doll, a baby doll dressed in a christening gown of exquisite needlework.

But she hardly saw the toy. Now that his back was to her, she was free to study him, free to examine the changes. It was partly his clothes, she thought as he squatted down to examine another doll. It was the first time she'd seen him in jeans, and they fit just as deliciously as everything else.

In fact, her first glimpse of him today, walking toward them from the house, had made her knees feel slightly weak. Good thing she hadn't still been up in the tree—she would have fallen out. She felt a little jelly-legged even now.

Along with those wonderful jeans, he wore cowboy boots and a white cotton shirt, collarless and open at the throat, exposing just enough dark chest hair to make her recall how he'd looked the time he'd taken off his sweatshirt after a run. Because frost was predicted for this evening, he'd pulled on a green-and-navy plaid flannel shirt that hung loose and unbuttoned over the white one, but the two inches of chest hair still dominated the scene.

He tilted his head, talking to the men, presenting his profile to Hilary. He hadn't shaved today, and the shadows along his upper lip and jaw contributed to the total, unnerving effect of rumpled intimacy.

"Do you think Marlene would like one of these for the baby?" He rose to his feet, holding out the christening doll.

Hilary blushed, certain he had seen her eyes roaming where they should not have. "Sure," she said quickly, trying to hide her embarrassment as well as her surprise that he would be so thoughtful toward Marlene. "But what if the baby isn't a girl?"

"What a sexist comment," he said, chuckling as he opened his wallet and counted out a great many bills. "Can't little boys have dolls?"

"No, sir," the oldest, most wizened old man behind the table spoke up firmly. "They sure as blazes cain't."

Conner laughed aloud at that and handed the money to the old man, who took it phlegmatically.

"All right, then. If it's a boy, Hilary, you can keep the doll." Conner held it out, the tiny wooden hands stretching toward Hilary with eerie supplication. "Here, hold her. If you're going to be her mother, you might as well get to know her right away."

She almost refused. Something in the silly scene unsettled her. Maybe it was the sight of Conner, who up until five minutes ago would have been at the top of her list of impossibly chauvinistic men, dangling the baby doll with no hint of self-consciousness. Or maybe, she thought, forcing herself to be more honest, she was paralyzed by a tension she recognized as quite sexual. A tension produced by thinking of Conner and babies in the same instant.

He frowned at her reproachfully. "What? No maternal instincts?" He grabbed her hand and brought it up to her chest, making a cradle out of the crook of her elbow. Then he nestled the doll up against her, its tiny face fitting perfectly in the hollow between her breast and upper arm. "There now," he said, stepping back to survey his efforts. "That's better."

"Well, Mr. Big Shot," a rough voice broke in. "Are you coming over here or not?"

Conner looked toward the voice, which came from a very tall, very thin, elderly man at the next stall. Like a cartoon mountain man, he wore a flannel hat and talked around the corncob pipe he held, unlit, between surprisingly white teeth.

"Or are you too good for your friends now that you own the ground we all walk on?"

Conner grinned and walked over to the booth, which was densely littered with small wooden objects and animals. "I don't own it yet, you old devil." He pushed some of the animals aside to clear a corner of the table and propped himself on the edge. "And if you don't keep your mouth shut I never will."

"I know, I know. Hush-hush and all that. Don't kid yourself, son. Everybody knows you're angling to buy this place. Word is they're planning to take you to the cleaners first."

Conner grimaced. "That's sure what it looks like."

But the grimace was superficial. Hilary was stunned by Conner's relaxed tone, and by the significance of the comments. So the deal wasn't signed yet. What, then, accounted for the change in his mood?

But there was no time to think about that. Conner was motioning her over.

"Hilary, come meet the insufferable Jules Avery, an old friend of mine. Call him Julie."

"Hi," she said, and readjusted the doll as she stepped forward, tucking it under her arm so that she carried it with exaggerated indifference. She smiled quizzically. "Julie?"

The man used the blade of a rather lethal-looking jackknife to tip his flannel hat. "Yes'm. When you're handy with a knife, it doesn't much matter what your nickname is, know what I mean?"

"Absolutely." Charmed, she shook his outstretched hand. She surveyed the hodgepodge of wood carvings displayed on the table, out of courtesy at first, but she soon realized that each object was a work of art. People, butterflies, jewelry, flowers, peacocks and dragons, lots of dragons—all finely detailed, but with the individuality seen only in things handmade.

She picked up a figure of a little boy. "Your work is magnificent," she said sincerely. "You truly have a gift."

"Yep, I guess I do." His voice was gruff, but his white teeth flashed even more brightly. He pointed his knife at Conner. "I like this one. I like her much better. She's got taste. Does that mean you've finally found some yourself?"

"How do you know she's got taste?" Maddeningly, Conner ignored the older man's question. Though Hilary kept her eyes trained on the carvings, she was prickling with curiosity. Better than whom? But Conner obviously wasn't going to elucidate. "Maybe she's just got manners."

Jules grunted disgustedly and turned back to Hilary. "I've known your friend here since he wasn't much bigger than that doll you've got there. Always was a stubborn cuss."

Hilary glanced up, shifting the doll nervously. "Really?"

"Yep." Jules leaned his straight chair back on two legs and worked it like a rocker. "I could've taught him carving, too, if he hadn't been so damn stubborn. He's got good hands."

Hilary managed not to turn her gaze to Conner's hands, but the effort left her short of breath. She squeezed her fingers around the shaft of an ornately carved letter opener and gave Jules a bright, interested look. She really did want to hear more. She could hardly imagine Conner as a child.

"Uh-huh, good hands, but too damn much stubborn pride," Jules went on. "You know, every piece of wood is destined to be something particular." He picked up a wooden star. "You see, this piece of wood just had to be a star. Now, I didn't much feel like carving a star, and I might never meet a single dern person who wants to buy a star. Tourists kinda go for farm animals, you know?"

He looked at the star with a resigned annoyance. "But it wouldn't have done me any good to try to make a cow out of it, 'cause it was meant to be a star. You follow me?"

Hilary smiled. "I guess so," she said. She sensed that Conner had grown very still. Irritated? Or just listening?

"Well, problem was this cocky whippersnapper always wanted to force something into the wood. He wasn't spoiled exactly, just willful. Couldn't stand letting the wood be in control, you know? If he wanted it to be a cow, then he'd just start whittling away, trying to make it *be* a cow. And maybe it would even look like a cow when he was done, but it was always a damn sorry cow, 'cause it was supposed to be a star.''

Hilary chuckled slightly, but she was acutely aware of Conner's tension. Jules and he seemed to be communicating on some level she didn't fully understand.

"See," Jules went on—he was looking at Hilary, but somehow she knew he was talking to Conner—"letting things be what they're supposed to be is something you gotta learn. And there are only two ways you can learn it. You can get old, like me. Or you can have it knocked into you by hitting enough bumpy spots along the road. Conner here was too young, and he'd never laid eyes on a bumpy spot. His road had been paved slick as glass.''

Finally Hilary looked at Conner and was surprised to see that his face was drawn tight, the circles under his eyes as dark as soot. Jules looked at him, too, a curiously sympathetic expression in his eyes.

"Though my guess is that you might do better if I handed you a chunk of mahogany today, mightn't you, son?''

Conner shook his head slowly, picking up a dragon and turning it over and over in his hands. "I don't know, Julie. I just don't know. But I'd try.''

"I heard about Tommy," Jules said, apparently the comment following quite logically to him. "That was a damn shame. Nice little kid.'' He watched the dragon writhe in Conner's hands. "But he wasn't really a little kid, was he? I hear he left a widow and a baby on the way."

Conner didn't answer, his gaze fixed on the dragon as it rhythmically twisted through his fingers. Hilary couldn't see his face, but a pulse labored in his temple. She jumped in before the silence could stretch too thin.

"That's right, Julie," she said. "Marlene and Tommy got married about three months before he died. The baby's due in a couple of months." She flicked a glance at Conner, but he hadn't looked up. "I'm Marlene's cousin—that's why I'm visiting."

Jules smiled. "Well, I'm glad you're here." He raised his voice, as if Conner had gone temporarily deaf. "Aren't you glad she's here, son? The lady's in harmony. Know what I mean? You could use some harmony."

Conner's eyes flicked up and met Hilary's in an expression of mutual skepticism. Harmony? She felt a sudden, inappropriate urge to laugh, and she knew he did, too. There hadn't been a single harmonious moment between them since she'd arrived. So much for Jules's folk wisdom.

But Jules had caught the shared glance, the ironic disbelief, and it clearly annoyed him.

"I don't mean in harmony with *you*, you dunderhead. I mean in harmony with herself. Nobody can be in harmony with *you* until you get your own head straightened out."

He pushed at Conner's elbow with impatient, whisking motions. "Now get off my table and let the paying customers have a chance. Go get the lady something to eat. And take that dragon with you. I never did like it. I read the wood wrong. I think it was probably supposed to be a jackass."

CHAPTER SEVEN

THEY WALKED several yards in silence, under a canopy of burnished maples. Someone was playing a dulcimer, a haunting ballad that Hilary half recognized. Maybe she should ask Conner what it was—that might be a good way to break the spell Jules Avery had cast.

She opened her mouth, but one glance at Conner, his hands in his pockets and his shoulders hunched defensively against the wind, changed her mind. She might not know the whole story of the two brothers, but she had understood enough of Jules's comments to realize that Conner must have found them troubling.

She looked away, not wanting to invade his privacy even by watching him. If he needed time to collect his thoughts, she could handle that. She wasn't afraid of a little silence.

And so they kept walking, passing a dozen booths, all offering beautiful crafts he didn't even notice. Soft quilts, graceful rockers, smiling dolls and cherry-wood dulcimers spilled across tables, magical in the lambent light, but he strode past, eyes clouded, seeing nothing. Hilary smiled a wordless apology to the disappointed artisans as she hurried by, only half a step behind him.

Gradually the maple canopy thickened, and the light grew almost crimson. Hilary shivered, pulling her jacket close, hugging the doll to her chest. It was getting late, and the fading afternoon sun couldn't penetrate this ruby vault.

"Cold?"

She glanced up, surprised he'd noticed. When had he returned to her world?

"A little," she admitted. "The wind's picked up, don't you think?"

Talk about stating the obvious! All around them leaves seemed to be leaping from the trees, hang gliding through the crisp air before sinking onto the path. His shoulders were dusted with leaves, and she knew hers must be, too.

"Goodness." She brushed at her jacket. "I'm a mess."

Brilliant! But she had to say something. He was looking at her, and she was very much afraid that he might...

He did.

"Come here," he said. As if it was the most natural thing in the world, he wrapped his arm around her shoulders and pulled her up against him, offering his body as protection.

"Better?" Ignoring her stiff resistance, he rubbed her arm slowly, sliding the cashmere of her jacket up and down against her skin. A thousand goose bumps rose and died away as his heat reached her.

"Yes," she said. "Much better, thanks."

And it was. Against her will, her muscles relaxed, lulled by the warmth and the rhythmic, almost hypnotic, stroking along her arm. *Careful now,* she told herself, holding her spine diligently erect. This wasn't an embrace. It was merely a courtesy. He didn't have a coat, so he'd lent her his arm.

"Isn't it about time to meet Marlene and Terri?" She hoped it was. And even if it wasn't, it seemed like a good idea to remind him—and herself—that this intimacy was temporary.

As she'd expected, hoped he would, he dropped his arm to check his watch, allowing her to edge an inch or two away. She clenched her teeth against the wind that rushed between them. No more coy shivering, she told herself. Not even if she froze to death.

"I guess it is." His voice was bland, not revealing whether he found the prospect pleasant or depressing. He scanned their surroundings quickly, making no attempt to put his arm around her again. "We're almost there, anyway. I've been smelling onion rings for five minutes now, haven't you?"

She nodded, but it was a lie. She hadn't been aware of anything except the feel of his hand on her arm. Taking a deep breath, she realized he was right. "Which way?"

"Just through here." He ducked between two booths and suddenly there they were, standing in the middle of the picnic area, where a dozen wooden tables were surrounded by junk-food stands of every description: fried dough, cotton candy, pizza, colas, french fries, hot dogs and, of course, the aromatic onion rings.

But Terri and Marlene were nowhere in sight.

"How about a hot chocolate while we wait?" Conner took her elbow impersonally, weaving through the crowds hunting for an empty table. "It might take off the chill."

"That would be nice," she said, though she loathed hot chocolate. She could at least wrap her hands around the cup and soak in its warmth that way.

While he did the ordering, she shared a picnic table with a family of five, the three children sloppily munching through sticky wads of cotton candy. But it was worth it, for the table was bathed in sunlight, and pulsing waves of heat streamed onto her back. Swiveling away from the kids, noisily sucking the pink sugar from their fingers, she tilted her face toward the rays, gratefully letting the numbness in her cheeks thaw.

"Hi! Sorry we're late!" With a clamor of voices and a rustle of packages, Terri and Marlene advanced upon her. The two young women produced such chaos that it took Hilary a couple of minutes to notice that Gil Lunsford was bobbing along in their wake.

"Hi, there, kiddo," she said, giving Terri a hug. "Hi, Gil." He smiled sheepishly, shifting several overstuffed bags from one arm to the other. "Marlene," Hilary added sternly, though she softened the scold with a quick kiss, "what did you do—buy one of everything you saw?"

"Just the good stuff. The girl stuff." Marlene dropped onto the bench finally vacated by the sticky family. "We didn't even *look* at the knives and tools and stuff."

Hilary sighed. "I knew I shouldn't have left you girls alone. Gil, how did you get dragged into this? And couldn't you do anything to dam the flood?"

"Not a thing," he said, but the beaming look he gave Marlene proved he hadn't even tried. "I just ran into them about an hour ago, and they were so loaded down I offered to be their pack mule."

Terri laughed. "Marlene was ready to hang bags from his ears. She bought hundreds of the most darling things for the baby. Wait till you see them."

Marlene began to rummage through the packages, eager to display her booty, but Hilary stopped her, pointing to a telltale pink spot on the table. "Not now. You don't want to get cotton candy on everything."

But that wasn't the only reason to wait. Eyeing the mound of purchases, Hilary couldn't help seeing them from Conner's perspective. He already believed Marlene was after the St. George money, and this new spurt of acquisitive greed would only confirm his suspicions.

Hilary sighed again. She loved Marlene dearly, but she'd be a lot easier to defend if she exercised a little restraint.

However, Hilary didn't have the heart to lecture anyone right now. Everyone seemed so merry, and besides, there was no need to embarrass Terri and Gil. She'd speak to Marlene about it later.

Still, her stomach tightened when she saw Conner coming toward them, a steaming cup of hot chocolate in each hand.

"Hello, ladies, Gil," he said pleasantly, setting the cups down in front of Hilary. He raised his brows at Gil's presence but, amazingly, seemed indifferent to the heap of purchases. "I didn't know you were here yet. I'll get some more."

"What is it?" Marlene peered down into Hilary's cup. "Oh, hot chocolate—goody. I'm freezing."

"Hot chocolate?" Terri grimaced and gave Hilary a quizzical look. "You don't drink hot chocolate, Hilary. You *hate* hot chocolate."

Hilary's cheeks flamed. "Terri..." she said quellingly.

But Conner had heard. "No problem," he assured the younger girl, who was looking stricken at her lapse of manners. "Someone else can drink it. I'll get Hilary a cup of coffee."

"It's not that there's anything wrong with it," Terri rambled on, trying to acquit herself. She was infuriatingly unaware of Hilary's efforts to shut her up. "It's just that the Gidgets always gave us hot chocolate, and now we can't even smell it without thinking of them."

Gil seemed confused. "The Gidgets?"

Terri laughed, that joyous, tinkling sound that Hilary usually loved to hear. Right now it made her skin crawl. Terri was going to tell the whole pathetic story.

"Oh, that's just what we called Daddy's secretaries. Gidget One, Gidget Two, you know, like in the movies. There were four of them, all unbelievably bubbly and kind of dumb, like Gidget. He married Gidget Four after he and Mother divorced.''

Gil's mouth was open. ''And they *all* gave you hot chocolate?''

''Yeah, whenever we came to the office. They were trying to make friends, you know, to get on Daddy's good side. They thought we liked hot chocolate.''

''Why?'' Conner asked, and he was looking straight at Hilary, expecting her, not her sister, to answer. Though everyone else seemed to find Terri's little story hilarious, Connor clearly saw something different in it, something darker.

''Because our father told them we did,'' Hilary said, her chin high. The story hadn't ever pained Terri the way it did her. Terri had been too young—she hadn't understood what a betrayal the Gidgets represented. ''He didn't know us very well, and I suppose he thought all kids liked hot chocolate.''

Hilary turned away quickly from the sympathy she saw in his eyes, setting her jaw and blinking back maudlin tears that should never have appeared.

She didn't need sympathy, especially not his. It was all years ago, and the old pain had left only one remnant: her vow never to allow any man to hurt her the way her father had hurt her mother. No man, no matter how handsome, no matter how blue-eyed and dimple-blessed, was going to get close enough to break her heart.

But Hilary still found herself fighting tears. Her internal struggle for equilibrium was so intense she almost didn't hear the plans the others were making until it was too late. Something about a bluegrass concert at sunset.

No, no, no. She couldn't, wouldn't stay out here for the entire evening, with Conner's too-knowing eyes studying her.

"Sorry, guys, I'm beat," she said firmly. "No concerts for me. But don't let me spoil things. I can grab a cab home."

"Nonsense," Conner broke in. "I was just counting myself out, too. Terri and Marlene can go with Gil. I'll take you." Though Marlene aimed one good pout Conner's way, Gil was so flatteringly eager to escort her that she didn't persist. Within minutes, Gil and his two dates had gathered up their things and said their goodbyes, anxious to be off to get good seats.

Watching them go, Hilary cursed herself for her rash decision. She should have been paying attention. She should *always* pay attention when Conner was around.

"Shall we?" Conner was holding out his hand. She looked at him, her stomach squirming with dread and... She had to be honest. The other emotion was anticipation. An entire evening alone with him? Suddenly she couldn't quite catch her breath.

And he, damn him, smiled, as if he knew all about the miserable ambivalence that tortured her, and enjoyed his knowledge. But even this malicious smile was maddeningly sexy, and her heart flopped like a leaf caught in a downdraft.

What was it she'd thought a while back—that this situation was like walking a tightrope over quicksand?

Well, she'd just tumbled off the tightrope.

"WOULD YOU LIKE to see Fire Falls?"

Conner slowed the car as they approached a fork in the road, and he cast an inquiring glance at her. "It's not the biggest falls in the area, but it's my favorite. It's part of Dragon's Creek Resort, too." He peered off to the west, where the sky burned a clear vermillion. "Tonight it'll be stunning."

She didn't know what to say. If she said yes, at least it postponed the moment when they would be in his house alone together. On the other hand, perhaps at home he would be distracted. Telephones to answer, contracts to read, dances to choreograph. Something might save her.

She seemed incapable of making the decision, but, autocrat that he was, he took her hesitation for assent, and without further discussion swerved to the right, away from the road that would have led them home.

This road was narrower and seemed to have been notched into the edge of a granite cliff. To her left a high wall of jagged boulders winked in the deepening sunset, but to her right, seemingly just inches from her door, the mountain sheered off disconcertingly. As she looked down, her stomach lurched. One careless twist of the wheel would take the road right out from under them.

But Conner was not a careless driver. Although he looked utterly relaxed, holding the wheel with one hand as if the cliff wasn't even there, he was clearly master of his machine, and the car responded obediently to every subtle nudge. Still, it would be a sickening plunge....

"Why do they call it Fire Falls?" she asked, as much to get her mind off the cliff as anything. After checking to see that her lock was engaged, she shifted slightly, so that her back was to the door. Out of sight, out of mind. She hoped.

"You'd have to see it from an airplane to fully appreciate the image," he answered, manipulating a hairpin curve quite casually. "Dragon's Creek is a long, serpentine creek, and it really does look like a dragon. It ends at Fire Falls, which looks like the dragon's mouth." He chuckled. "A very irritable dragon, breathing about 150 gallons of firewater a second."

"Sounds impressive," she said. Almost as impressive as his driving. For an instant it had seemed as if they were going to drive straight off the mountain, and then, with precise timing, he had made the turn. She swallowed, reminded of the way she had felt on her first roller-coaster ride.

She was immensely relieved when after only a mile or so he pulled off, nosing the car into the beginning of a dirt path.

"It's quicker to walk from here," he said, pocketing the keys. "If you're up to it."

She nodded, though she eyed the overgrown, steep path in front of them with some concern.

He followed her gaze and read her mind. "It's not as bad as it looks." Twisting around, he grabbed a leather windbreaker for himself from the back seat and tossed her an oversize Irish-knit sweater. "You might want to wear this, instead of that jacket, though," he suggested. "It's cold by the falls."

Obediently—did anyone dare behave any other way with this man?—she tugged the sweater over her head and opened her door, stepping out into the frosty evening. They hadn't come far from the busy festival, but it might have been another world. It was so quiet, except for the whistle and twitter of evening birds and somewhere not too far away the rumble of falling water.

They met at the front of the car, and with a smile, he checked her appearance.

"Too big, of course, but it'll do." Reaching behind her head he pulled her hair out of the collar slowly, the long strands tickling her neck as he dragged them free. He lifted first one arm, then the other, to roll back the sweater's sleeves, which had been hanging over her hands. He looked down at her legs. The hem of the sweater came to her knees. "You won't trip over the darn thing, will you?"

"I'm fine," she said tersely, wishing he'd stop touching her. She wouldn't trip over the sweater, but if he didn't get his hands off her she might not be able to walk at all.

"Okay, let's go." He took her hand and led her onto the darkening path. "It's slippery in places, so be careful."

He was quite right. Though at the outset she resented being led around like a child, after the first time she lost her footing and nearly slid back down to the car, she was glad to cling to his hand. The path *was* as bad as it looked, quite steep in places and the mossy ground slippery as ice. Only pride and the ever-louder sound of roaring water kept her going. The falls must be near, though she couldn't see any signs of it yet.

Suddenly Connor left the path and, reaching both hands around her waist, hoisted her up onto a small ridge.

And there, right in front of them, was Fire Falls. She let out a small gasp of wonder, unable to believe her eyes.

It was, indeed, like looking at a cascade of fire. Tumbling over a massive ledge and plunging at least fifty feet, the falls caught the light from the sunset so perfectly that the water was a spectacular golden-red. At the base lay a wide pool, boiling where the waterfall poured into it, but spreading out with an eerie calm, like a vat of melted rubies.

"Oh," she murmured, but she could barely hear her own voice over the thundering water. "Oh, my God, it's magnificent."

His hands were still wrapped around her waist, steadying her on the moss-rimmed ridge, and he nudged her toward a wide granite slab. She took small, hesitant steps, leaning heavily against him to keep her balance, and at last sank gratefully onto the smooth rock.

Propping himself against the rise of earth behind him, he positioned her in front of him so that she sat between his legs, her back against his chest. His arms closed around her protectively, and she welcomed the embrace, which seemed a promise that he wouldn't let her fall. They were so close, so intoxicatingly close, to the rumbling, crashing flood, and she was both exhilarated and afraid.

His lips touched her ear. "Do you like it?" he asked, and each word was warm and clear.

She nodded, beyond words. It was the most thrilling sight she'd ever seen. Every inch of her tingled, from her head, which somehow had fallen back against his shoulder, to her feet, which were tucked up against her thighs. His legs tightened around her, and she nodded again, hoping he understood.

His arms were crossed over her chest, his hands cupping her upper arms, and he began to stroke her, warming her as he had done at the festival, sliding his palms slowly up and down from shoulder to elbow. Her heart, which had already been racing, pumped faster, harder, until she could feel it in her cheeks.

The musky smell of his jacket teased her nostrils. Under that, the flannel of his outer shirt smelled deliciously of pine—it had spent much time, she thought, in the woods.

Shutting her eyes, she breathed deeply, as if she were an animal who comprehended the world only through scent. Beneath the musky leather and piney flannel was the man himself, more complicated, more primitive, more stirring.

Strange how comfortably they fit together. Her head rested naturally in the small hollow between his upper arm and the pectoral muscle. Very like the way the doll's head had fit her own body, she remembered dreamily. Wasn't it one of nature's miracles how bodies were made to merge? Mother and child, man and woman.

A nagging voice told her it was a crude miracle at best—beasts accomplished the same mindless joining all the time. Is that what she wanted? A purely physical linking that was about as meaningful as the nesting of spoons in a drawer?

But the voice was weak and could barely be heard. Soon she heard nothing but the soft whoosh of his breath against her ear and the insistent roar of the falls. And then there was her heartbeat, which had suddenly become a loud pounding in her throat. Why was he doing this? Why was she letting him? This felt like a lover's caress, but they weren't lovers.

He would be such a wonderful lover, though, her traitorous mind insisted. She'd known that from the start. Now, through Jules's eyes, she had glimpsed the heart and passion within him. And he had good hands....

She shivered, and he pulled her closer. Oh, this was such delicious madness. All day she'd been on her guard. Sensing the danger, she'd thrown a protective wall up around herself, a skill she'd perfected over the years. Hiding there, she had believed she was safe.

Somehow, though, he had sneaked through. Some chink she hadn't suspected, some weakness she hadn't glimpsed, had allowed him in. And now she couldn't push him out. She didn't even want to, and that was the part that frightened her most.

She shivered again.

"Too cold?"

Mutely she shook her head, inadvertantly rubbing her cheek against his unshaven jaw. Shielded by his big body, she was warm, though a frigid spray from the falls blew toward them, misting their faces and beading their clothes with tiny, glistening pearls.

"Good." His hands moved up to her shoulders, and he began to knead them until she was so warm she began to melt, like sugar in the sun. She couldn't have lifted her head if she'd tried.

But she *should* have tried. When she didn't resist, the character of his touch changed: he passed without a word from succor to seduction. In an act of frank and unvarnished sensuality, his hands carressed her exposed throat, slipping two cool fingers up behind her ears.

It was something akin to hypnotism, she thought, from a distant place. She closed her eyes, mesmerized by the uncharted, deeply erotic path the two exploring fingers followed, and still she didn't protest. With growing confidence, his hands slid inside the neck of her sweater, traced the line of her collarbone and finally came to rest on the pulse that beat in the hollow just below her throat.

She swallowed convulsively and knew his cool fingers could feel it, could feel her quickened breath as she anticipated his next move. She should stop him now, while she was still able.

But he surprised her. As though sensing her resistance, he pulled his hands out and, instead, ran them over her sweater, allowing her the modesty of the thick wool.

But it might as well have been gossamer. She felt everything, every inch his hands traveled until they found the gentle swell of her breasts, which puckered, tingling helplessly at the touch. Perhaps he couldn't tell, she thought with muddled embarrassment, through all that wool....

But of course he could. His fingers never fumbled, closing unerringly around the sensitive peaks. She thought she made a sound, but the falls swept it away. Oh, yes, they were good hands, intuitive hands, probing first with a reverent touch that conveyed a blind, speechless wonder; then nipping gently, anticipating the very moment when she began to long for more of the exquisite stinging.

She sighed, a deep exhale that spoke of a profound abandon. Her legs relaxed, uncurling slowly, her heels sliding from their tucked position all the way down the smooth granite to the edge of the rock.

Sensing the emptiness, the momentary void where the secure granite ended and the steep slope began, she was vaguely afraid. Without thinking, responding only to mindless need, she reached up to clutch his shoulders, anchoring herself as if she feared she would lose control entirely.

That seemed to be the sign he was waiting for. His hands became more intimate, searching ever lower to discover every curve and hollow. A dangerous sinking dragged at her midsection, as though something had captured her and was pulling her down. She felt a moment of piercing panic.

And then there was only an ungovernable turbulence. Sensations she had never felt before writhed inside her, undulating, arcing and plunging, and she could scarcely keep her balance. She was riding the dragon, she thought incoherently, slipping relentlessly toward the searing fire of his mouth. "Hilary." Conner's breath came hot against her neck as his fingers grew more urgent, rougher—pushing, circling, tugging in frustration at the barriers of wool and denim.

She moaned. The dragon was in control now, and with a cry she arched back against Conner's chest, trying to hold on. The blood was running to her legs, until she was numb everywhere except the places his hands touched her. She dug her fingers into the hard muscles of his shoulders and cried out as the fire licked at her feet.

"Let go, Hilary," he whispered. "Just let it happen."

"Oh," she gasped. God, she mustn't fall. If she did, she was lost. She wouldn't let it happen.

And for an instant it seemed she would win. For an instant, in that flickering moment when she dangled over the void, everything seemed to stop. The falls froze in its endless descent, the wind hung poised and breathless in the sky. Even the blood stalled in her veins.

But he moved his hands one last time and even her desperate willpower wasn't enough to prevent it. She began to fall.

"Conner," she cried as she and the dragon and the waterfall became one—one savage, roaring, shivering cataclysm of sensation. "No!"

She fell and fell, and there was no bottom. There was only Conner. His shoulders. His hands.

And his voice, low against her neck. "Oh, yes, sweetheart," he murmured. "Yes."

CHAPTER EIGHT

THEY DROVE BACK to the house in utter silence. All the fire had been leeched from the sky, turning the world, even the falls, an unrelieved black. Conner wanted to say something, but Hilary's refusal to meet his eyes stopped the words in his throat. Though their intimacy had gone no further—the rock was too precarious and public for that—still, he knew he had gone too far. She was furious.

And, damn him for a fool, it was all his fault. What an adolescent jerk he'd been! He didn't usually rush things like such an inept baboon, but the feel of her body under his hands had driven him slightly mad.

Madness. That was definitely the word. If he'd been halfway sane, he would have seen what a mistake it was. This kind of thing was, obviously, shockingly, new to her. He had no idea what her experience was, but he was quite sure that if she'd ever taken a lover it had been the *wrong* lover.

And that was a tragedy. How selfish could the other men in her life have been? He squeezed the steering wheel, remembering with gut-twisting clarity how amazingly responsive she'd been—even as she'd resisted. But it had frightened her, that quick and total loss of control. She wasn't ready; she didn't trust him enough. She didn't, he somehow sensed, even trust *herself* enough.

Oh, God, if only he'd waited!

If they had been really making love, it would have been so different. In the safety of that reciprocal honesty, she wouldn't have had to fight her responses. She would have known that he was as vulnerable as she. She would have learned that, in the act of loving, each lover tasted power and each lover tasted fear.

Instead, he had left her feeling embarrassed and manipulated. She stared out the window, withdrawing from him, from the man who had engineered and then watched her humiliation as if it were a peepshow.

Oh, Hilary, he groaned inwardly, wishing he could show her how wrong she was. If only she knew how close he'd been to losing control himself. When they'd heard the other sightseers approaching the ridge, he'd hardly been able to stand up. Every step back down the cliff had been physical agony.

It helped a little to know that Hilary had found it difficult, too. She had managed to compose her face, but her legs kept betraying her. They were as unsteady as rubber, and she'd clutched at trees to keep from falling on the way down.

Finally he allowed himself the luxury of a small, internal smile. The night wasn't over yet. They were almost home. *One more mile, Hilary...* And then he'd make it up to her.

He covered the mile in record speed. As they drove up, the house was ablaze with lights, and in the glow it cast he could see Hilary's face clearly for the first time. Guilt stabbed at him again. She was so deathly pale, except where stains of red slashed across her cheekbones, stains that deepened when she realized he was watching her.

Ducking her head, she gathered up her jacket and purse, her movements stiff and restrained, looking like a bad actress trying to project nonchalance. She let her hair fall protectively over her face, apparently unaware that one torn leaf still clung to it like a jewel. With difficulty, he stopped himself from reaching out to touch it.

"Hilary," he began, not knowing what he was going to say, just knowing he couldn't let her rush into the house without his saying something. Could he say he was sorry? But he wasn't, not the way she wanted him to be. He wasn't sorry that he'd begun to make love to her. He was only sorry that he hadn't been able to do it right.

"Hilary, look at me." Maybe she could see the truth now, here in these overly bright lights. Maybe she could see that what had happened on the rock had been meant as a giving, not a taking.

But she wouldn't look. "I'm tired," she said to the window, settling her jacket over her arm. "I just need to get some sleep."

"No," he said, reaching out to catch her arm. But she was too quick. She'd already opened the door, and his hand merely brushed the lapel of her jacket before closing over empty air.

She was climbing the steps to the front door when it swung wildly open. Terri stood there, hands against her face. Because she was silhouetted against the light, it took him a minute to realize she'd been crying.

"Thank God," Terri cried, choking on the words. "You're here." She held out her hands, begging for comfort from her big sister.

"What is it?" Hilary ran the rest of the way, dropping her jacket unnoticed on the stairs. Her voice was full of barely controlled terror. "What's the matter, honey?"

"It's Marlene," Terri sobbed, grabbing Hilary's hands and casting an anguished look toward Conner. "You need to go to the hospital. Gil drove her there. She was bleeding."

Hilary spun around, her pale face fading to white. "Conner," she said, her voice faltering. "Marlene—"

"I heard." As fear and pain, two emotions that were destructive to intelligent action, sped toward him like poisoned arrows, he gripped the stair railing and took a deep breath. Closing his eyes for a split second, he switched off his feelings, a defensive technique he'd learned so long ago he'd forgotten when and where. Then he opened his eyes and, now no more than a robot going through the motions, turned to Terri. "When did they leave?"

The girl shook her head, trying to remember. "I don't know for sure. It seems like forever. We didn't know where you were. They made me wait for you here, so I could tell you." She rubbed her eyes, as if attempting to clear tears from her mental vision. "It was just before it got really dark. Maybe an hour ago?" Her face crumpled. "I'm just not sure."

"That's all right. You did fine," Conner said briefly, then took the stairs two at a time back to the car. "Wait here," he called to the two women, who still stood frozen on the front porch. "I'll call you when I find out what's happening."

"Conner!" Suddenly, as if galvanized by the roar as he gassed the engine, Hilary dragged Terri out of the doorway and down the stairs. "We're coming with you."

"No," he said without thinking. He didn't know how long his robot facade would last. His defenses, like everything else, had been worn down by the siege of restless nights, of fighting dragons even in his sleep. If Tommy's baby— He broke off the thought. If anything had gone wrong, would he have the strength to keep the pain at bay? No, if he had to face bad news, he wanted to be alone.

"We're coming," Hilary said, and her voice allowed no argument. "We're family."

Family. Ironically, only now that he had none did he fully appreciate the power of that word. Family. Instantly he saw how wrong he'd been. He had no right to shut Hilary out just to protect himself. Suppose something happened to Marlene—Hilary would never be able to live with herself if she hadn't been there. He, of all people, should understand that.

"Get in," he said, his voice rough as he leaned over to push open her door. But she hadn't been waiting for his permission. She'd already herded Terri into the back seat, and was ready to jump into the front.

As he pulled away, tires squealing, Hilary reached her left arm over the seat and clutched her sister's hand.

"It'll be all right," she said, but in answer Terri only sobbed softly.

Conner watched the road, concentrating on negotiating the risky turns at the highest speed he could safely manage, but he could see Hilary out of the corner of his eye.

"Don't worry." Her voice was the low, gentling one she always used with Terri. He tried not to listen—the voice was insinuating itself under his mechanical facade. And he needed that facade. It had seen him through every crisis of his life, had allowed him to "keep his heart out of it" and had won him his father's admiration.

But his father was gone. Tommy, who had worn his heart on his sleeve, refusing to become a robot just to impress his father, was gone. And now Tommy's child...

"Everything will be fine, I'm sure of it." Hilary's tone was like a blanket, warm and comforting, wrapping itself around the fear. But the tone wasn't for her little sister this time. She wasn't looking at Terri.

She was looking at him.

FROM HER RESTLESS PERCH on the edge of a chair, Hilary stared at the beige walls of the hospital waiting room, hating them. She hated the comfortable seats,

too, seats designed for frightened, brokenhearted
people to wait in endlessly. She hated those double
doors that didn't open. She hated that doctor who,
minute after minute, just wouldn't come through
them. Standing up, she prowled to the window, which
looked out over a flat roof. God, she hated hospitals.

They'd been here an hour, though they'd been told
that the doctor was with Marlene and would be out to
talk to them momentarily. Gil had fussed and fumed
and complained to the nurses' station twice, until
Conner had sent him out for coffee just to shut him
up. Terri had curled up in one of the comfortable
chairs, her head on her arm, her eyes red-rimmed and
a well-used tissue in her hand.

And Conner... Hilary looked over at him, standing at the edge of the waiting room, one shoulder
propped against the wall, staring blankly down the
brightly lit corridor. She didn't know how to describe
Conner. It was as if he simply wasn't... there.

"Mr. St. George?" Miraculously the double doors
opened, and a young, white-coated man stepped
through them. The doctor! Hilary and Terri both
rushed to Conner's side just as he identified himself.
Dr. Schaffman, the emergency-room doctor. His eyes
were dark brown and kindly, but, oh, he was so
young!

The doctor smiled at the women, then turned back
to Conner. "Mrs. St. George is going to be fine. So is
the baby." Terri made a small choking sound, and
Hilary, filled with relief, slipped an arm around her
shoulders.

Conner's face didn't change at all. If he felt relief, he didn't show it. But then he hadn't shown anxiety, either. Everything was locked away, far, far away.

"And the bleeding?" he asked in a quiet monotone.

"The bleeding wasn't very serious, and it's stopped completely." The doctor smiled again, reassuringly. "It's not terribly uncommon at this late stage of a pregnancy, but it frightened her. She's at least seven months along, which means the baby would probably be fine even if she did go into labor, but of course it's better if we can keep that from happening."

He gave Conner a man-to-man look. "We called in her own doctor, Dr. Pritchard. He just arrived, so it's going to be a little while before we know whether he wants to have her admitted."

"Admitted?" Hilary's voice was tight. "I thought you said she was fine."

Dr. Schaffman touched her forearm gently. He might be young, but he had a soothing manner. "She is. But she does need to stay in bed and get plenty of rest, and she certainly shouldn't do anything strenuous. Dr. Pritchard might decide it's easier to keep an eye on her here."

"Where is she?" Hilary had been waiting for Conner to ask that question, but it appeared he wasn't going to. "Can we see her?"

"Not until Dr. Pritchard is finished examining her. In fact, since it's getting so late, it might be better if some of you went home. Get some rest yourselves. I promise you, there's no emergency tonight."

To Hilary's dismay, Conner nodded, as though the idea was eminently sensible. "Why don't you find Gil and see if he can take you home? I'll wait here."

"No," she said firmly. "We'll wait, too."

"There's really no need," the doctor interjected. He smiled over at Terri. "And *this* young lady looks all done in."

Embarrassed, Terri tried to rally. "I'm fine," she denied with a smile that didn't persuade anyone. Her eyes were weary, and her skin was gray.

Still, though her heart went out to her sister, Hilary couldn't bring herself to leave. It wasn't because of Marlene, really. She knew that Conner would take good care of her, and besides, Dr. Schaffman's reassurances seemed sincere.

No, it was something else, something about Conner himself. She looked at him dubiously. Something about his extreme control was abnormal. Maybe if she hadn't glimpsed how much this baby meant to him she would have believed his iron-man act, but she had.

But what could she say? "I can't go because I'm worried about Conner?" Looking at him now, the picture of complete calm, she knew how ridiculous that would sound. But it's an act, she wanted to scream. Look at his eyes—the blue is almost gone. And his mouth—that's not his mouth. His real mouth is full and mobile and warm and . . .

"All right, then, good." The doctor seemed to assume the decision was made. "Mr. St. George, if you'll go to the front desk, there are some papers you need to sign. And there are a few other things I want to talk to you about."

LESS THAN AN HOUR LATER, Hilary knelt in front of the fireplace at Conner's house, stacking thick, sweet-smelling logs on the grate. She seemed to carry a chill inside her that even the central heating couldn't dispel, and her fingers were clumsy as she tried to strike a match. When it finally fizzed into life, she held it to the kindling, then sat back to watch as the fire crawled slowly through the splinters of wood, consuming them effortlessly on its way toward the logs.

Terri drowsed on the sofa behind her. She had refused to go to bed until she saw Marlene, so Hilary had insisted she lie down here, where she could easily hear the telephone or her cousin's arrival, whichever came first.

Surprisingly, Hilary herself wasn't tired at all. She felt full of nervous energy, which she had tried to work off by bustling around, procuring pillows and blankets for Terri, readying Marlene's room, brewing cinnamon tea and, finally, laying the fire.

Conversation had been desultory since Gil had dropped them off, then had ceased altogether as Terri's eyes closed and her breathing grew deep and even. Good, Hilary thought, watching the firelight play across her sister's peaceful face. Terri's flight back to college was scheduled for the morning, and she needed some rest.

As the logs finally surrendered to the insistent red tongues of fire, Hilary settled herself on the floor, her elbow on the sofa near Terri's feet, her head resting on her hand. Waves of heat pulsed toward her, caressing her face; eventually the chill dissipated and she relaxed. Her eyes drifted shut, and the fire's dancing shadows, which she could sense even through her closed lids, were like pieces of a dream.

A shrill ringing tore into the dream. The telephone.

Terri had already raised herself to a half-sitting position, her eyes vaguely unfocused but blinking hard by the time Hilary got to the phone.

"Hello?"

"Hi." It was Conner. Hilary sank to the arm of the sofa and gripped the receiver tightly. "I just wanted to let you know we're coming home. Dr. Pritchard says she's fine."

"Yes," she said stupidly. "Yes, that's good. I'm glad."

"Is everything all right there?"

"Fine," she answered. "I've got her room ready and some hot tea. I've started a fire." Lord, how dumb she sounded, like a child who'd done her chores and now wanted a pat on the head. But she was so glad he was coming home, so glad. Wasn't that ironic? Just a few hours ago she had been desperate to get away from him, and now she could hardly wait for his return. She shifted the phone to the other hand. Her feelings for Conner St. George were certainly mixed up.

"Thank you," he said politely. "Well, we'll be home soon."

They said their goodbyes like two cordial strangers, and with a strangely hollow feeling, Hilary turned to reassure Terri, who was biting her lips in impatient anxiety.

"They're coming home," she said, but the words had a poignant sound. She tried to buoy up her voice, make it more cheerful. "Marlene must be doing fine if Dr. Pritchard said she could come home."

Terri sank back onto the sofa with a sigh.

"Thank God," she said heavily, but she didn't seem as relieved as Hilary had expected. While Hilary made cups of tea for each of them, Terri stared at the fire, sighing once or twice more. It was as if she carried some other burden, Hilary thought, and was looking for a way to put it down.

Eventually Terri spoke, without taking her gaze from the fire. "I've been wondering about something." She shifted her feet, tucking them under her, and sipped her tea. "Why did Dr. Schaffman want Conner to sign Marlene's hospital papers?"

Something in her voice, some small note of anxiety, came through, and Hilary looked at her with curiosity. Why should that worry her? But the fire's shadows distorted Terri's face, and Hilary couldn't read her expression.

"I don't know," she responded halfheartedly. She must have donned a disaster mentality—she was imagining problems everywhere. Her thoughts returned to Conner and Marlene. What would they talk about during the intimacy of the car ride home, she wondered? Her own ride with Conner had been so miserably silent... "It was probably just something about the insurance, about the bill—stuff like that."

"Yeah, but why Conner? Does he pay her doctor bills?" Terri finally looked over at her sister, and now the tension in her voice was unmistakable. Hilary had not imagined it.

"Of course." Hilary raised her brows, surprised that the subject should rouse any emotion at all. "Who did you think paid them? Don't you remember all those letters we got from Marlene complaining about how she didn't have any money and how stingy her brother-in-law was being?"

"Yeah, but... well, I guess I thought she was exaggerating. You know how she is...." Terri paused, chewing her lower lip. "I guess I thought she had *some* money."

"I don't think so. I think Conner is taking care of everything."

Terri stared at the floor, her brow furrowed, her face strained. "When somebody else is paying your bills," she said slowly, as if she were choosing her words carefully, "does that mean that the doctor has to tell them everything about you?"

Hilary frowned. The question seemed strange, and yet Terri's tone implied it was very important. "What do you mean, everything?"

"You know." Putting her cup in her lap, Terri toyed with the fringe of her blanket, looking wretched. "Doctors are like priests or something, aren't they? They're never supposed to reveal the things you tell them. But if someone else is paying the doctor for you, well, does that give them the right to know everything?''

Something was going on here. "Terri," Hilary said sternly, setting her cup on the end table and moving in front of her sister so she could better see her face. "What are you talking about? Has Marlene told you something?"

"No, not really," Terri said hotly, but her face was pale, and she didn't seem to want to meet Hilary's eyes.

"Then what is all this about doctor confidentiality and the seal of the confessional?" She reached out and took Terri's arm in a firm grip. "Terri, if there's anything wrong with Marlene, Conner should know about it."

Terri didn't answer. A wash of cold fear doused Hilary suddenly as another possibility occurred to her, and her heart pumped erratically. It couldn't be. It just couldn't be. Fate would never be so cruel.

"Oh, my God," she said, her hand tightening. "Is there anything wrong with the baby?"

But Terri was shaking her head emphatically. "No, no, nothing like that. I'm sure the baby is fine, and Marlene, too. It's just something she said." Terri wriggled her arms, as if trying to relax Hilary's biting grip. "Hey, ease up. Even if Marlene *had* told me something, I couldn't tell you. And she didn't, I'm just guessing, honestly. It's not important and, ouch, you're hurting me."

Chagrined, Hilary let go and stood up, trying to calm herself. She hadn't meant to frighten Terri, but the thought that something might be wrong with the baby... She ran her fingers through her hair, realizing she hadn't brushed it since her trip to the waterfall. She must look wild. It had been a long day, full of conflicting, troubling emotions, and she was letting herself get overwrought.

Her sister's secret might be nothing more mysterious than the fact that the baby had been conceived before the marriage. She might not realize that Hilary already knew that, and it might loom large in her innocent mind.

But, whatever it was, she shouldn't be grilling Terri like this. The poor girl probably didn't know what to do, caught between Marlene's demanding friendship and her older sister's inquisition.

"Sorry, honey," she said meekly, and rested her back against the mantel, trying to force her heart rate back to normal.

She would have to find out eventually, of course, just to be sure everything was all right. But she wouldn't try to pry it out of Terri anymore. When Marlene was a little stronger, she and Hilary would have a talk. As long as whatever it was wasn't life-threatening, it could wait a day or so.

"You know, Hilary—" Terri hunched forward, toying with her cup nervously "—you *can* be a bit overwhelming."

Hilary felt terrible. "I'm sorry, kiddo," she said again. "I didn't mean to hurt you, and I really shouldn't have put you on the spot like that. You don't have to betray any secrets."

"No, I mean all the time." Terri glanced up at her older sister, and her sweet eyes were grave. "You're always so—I don't know—so *perfect*. You never seem to make mistakes, and you're always so disappointed when the rest of us can't live up to your standards." She smiled sheepishly. "That can really make a person feel like dirt."

Hilary was stunned—and hurt. She had never heard her sister say such things, had never even guessed that she thought them. Did Terri really see her in such an unflattering light—judgmental, unyielding, righteous?

She sat down on the sofa next to her sister. "Honey," she said, and her fingers were shaking as she took Terri's cup and put it on the table, before enfolding her sister's hands in hers. "I've never been disappointed in you, never. All those things that happened were not your fault. I never blamed you."

Terri made a small frustrated sound and shook Hilary's hands in exasperation.

"That's exactly what I mean," she said, her voice tight. "You can't accept that I made mistakes. But I did, Hilary. A lot of what happened *was* my fault. I didn't know he was still married, but I did know he was too old for me. And I knew I shouldn't have been sleeping with him. I knew I was in over my head."

Hilary made soothing sounds, but Terri wouldn't be interrupted. Obviously she'd held in her feelings for so long they'd finally burst forth like steam from a kettle.

"And you know what was the worst? It wasn't when I found out he was married. It wasn't even when I got the subpoena to testify at the divorce hearing. It was when I realized I was going to have to tell *you* about it."

Tears pooled along the rims of her eyes, and her voice quavered. "*That* was when it all seemed unendurable, when I thought I just couldn't go on." She touched the scar on the inside of her wrist. "That's when *this* happened. Because I just couldn't face you. You were going to be so disappointed in me. I knew you would never understand."

Never understand? What was she saying? Hilary had never been unkind to Terri, never condemned her, never done anything but try to help her. Hilary could hardly breathe. The flue must need cleaning—smoke was wafting toward her, making her eyes sting and fill with tears.

"You see," Terri said, as if she'd heard Hilary's internal protestations, "it wasn't that you were mean to me. You've never been mean. It was just that, after Daddy, you always tried to teach me to be strong, not to let any man break my heart. And you were so strong. How could you understand that I'd let a man make a fool of me?" Hilary winced again. It wasn't the smoke making her cry. The tears were real, brought on by Terri's uncannily accurate portrayal of her. Every word she said had the awful, bludgeoning impact of truth. Hilary's head fairly reverberated with it.

Although she'd supported and comforted her little sister, she had not understood. She had rather smugly considered herself the strong Fairfax woman, the one who was too smart to get caught with her barriers down. So self-satisfied. So self-righteous.

What a joke! She'd actually been the most ignorant of them all. She had understood nothing. She had possessed no inkling of how enslaving passion could be, how it could sing in your veins, drowning out the voice of common sense. She could not have imagined how addictive it was to touch the body of the man you loved, and to have him touch yours....

Until today.

The tears rolled freely down her face. Now she knew. Now, like her mother and sister before her, she was in love. And in true Fairfax tradition, she had chosen to love unwisely. Hopelessly. And quite uncontrollably. She had fallen in love with a man who was, God help her, just like her father, a tough businessman who didn't really care about her. Both of them, her father and Conner St. George, loved control, loved power, far more than they could ever love a human being.

She opened her lips, letting the tears run into her mouth, hot and salty against her tongue. In love with Conner? Another tear slid in. It was insanity. It was as destructive as what Terri had tried to do—a form of *emotional* suicide.

Yet she knew that if he came to her again and kissed her and offered her even one night, she would take that night. Not because it was sensible or because it spared her any pain, but because it was one last, life-affirming moment of joy. And because her body, which could not think or analyze but could only feel, demanded it.

Someday she would tell her sister all of this, would admit that she had been wrong, so wrong, to judge her. But she couldn't tell her now. She had only just found the courage to admit it to herself.

Instead, she leaned over and kissed her. "I'm sorry," she said. "I've been a fool." That, at least, was the truth. A fool on all counts.

"No." Terri shook her head, wrapping her arms around Hilary's neck. "You've been the best big sister anyone could have," she declared loyally, sounding close to tears herself. Hilary clung to her, letting her unconditional love wash soothingly over the new, agonizing wound—the wound she would carry for the rest of her life.

She barely heard the key turn in the lock, but suddenly the front door opened, and Conner was there, Marlene by his side. His hand was under her elbow, supporting her. And for once in her life, Marlene truly needed it—she looked fragile, exhausted and thoroughly subdued.

Disengaging Terri's arms, Hilary stood up, wiping the dampness from her cheeks quickly and clearing her throat. It wouldn't do for Marlene to know she'd been crying. Everything was going to be fine, and everyone had to stay upbeat.

"Hi!" she exclaimed, hugging her cousin tightly. "Come on in and let me help you get settled in bed. Conner, I—"

But she never got the chance to finish. The telephone rang, and Conner strode across the room to pick it up. She watched him for a moment, amazed that his stride was as crisp and controlled as it had been this morning. His eyes were shadowed, and his mouth was still a little too tight, but otherwise he seemed unaffected by the grueling day.

Hilary stood, transfixed, waiting for him to finish his conversation, but Marlene made an irritated sound and began walking toward her room. "Always business," she muttered angrily.

Coming to, Hilary put her hand out to help her, but Marlene brushed it away.

"I just want to be alone for a few minutes," she said, placing her hand on the wall to steady herself. "I need to clean up." She gave Hilary an unsteady, apologetic smile. "Come see me later, okay? Right now I really want to be alone."

"All right," Hilary said, trying not to disapprove of Marlene's snappish behavior. Marlene was clearly upset—more upset than she should be. After all, Dr. Pritchard had said everything was fine.

Suddenly she remembered Terri's puzzling questions, and she watched Marlene's departing figure with a growing sense of dread.

"Terri," she called softly, so that Conner couldn't hear them over his conversation. Terri rose obediently and joined Hilary in the hall. "What's the matter with Marlene?"

"I don't know," Terri said, keeping her voice low, too. She stopped a couple of feet behind Hilary, as though deciding it wasn't wise to go any farther. She started chewing her lower lip again and was tearing at the tissue she still held in her hand. "But...when you go in to talk to Marlene, remember what I said."

Hilary went cold again. "Which part?"

Terri must have worried her lip raw by now. "You know." She swallowed hard before she went on. "The part about not making her feel like dirt."

Hilary frowned, feeling an unpleasant stab of anxiety. She could hear the low rumble of Conner's telephone conversation. Who was he talking to at this hour? "I thought you said it wasn't important."

"It probably isn't." The tortured tissue disintegrated, falling like snow onto the carpet. "I hope it's not."

But Hilary's anxiety had burgeoned into fear. This wasn't a problem of an embarrassingly early due date, she realized. Terri wasn't, after all, that innocent and naive. Though in Hilary's eyes Terri would always be a vulnerable younger sister, she was actually a grown woman who had known despair and could tell the real thing from its shadow.

No. This *was* important. Hilary saw it in Terri's eyes. Something was very, very wrong.

CHAPTER NINE

WHEN HILARY KNOCKED on her door ten minutes later, Marlene was sitting up in bed, looking pale and tragic. Her mascara was pooled under her blue eyes, giving her the bruised look of an assault victim.

"How are you feeling?" Hilary embraced her gently and sat on the edge of the bed, guiltily aware that what she really wanted to do—wretched coward that she was—was flee from this room and whatever explosive secret Marlene might have. She was feeling emotionally battered herself.

"Horrible." Marlene's eyes filled with tears, which spilled over and ran in mascara-gray rivulets down her cheeks. What a pitiful trio the Fairfax women made, Hilary thought with an attempt at wry detachment. All three of them sitting in this beautiful house, bawling their eyes out.

But she didn't feel detached. She felt sick and much too tired to face more bad news. Patting Marlene's hand, she murmured something soothing, all the while praying that Marlene would wait until tomorrow to detonate her explosives. "Oh, Hilary—" Marlene clutched at her hand "—I really need to talk to you."

Heart plummeting, Hilary nodded mutely, accepting the inevitable. Marlene wasn't going to wait. Resolutely folding her own pain away, she tried to look loving and strong.

"I'm here," she said softly. "Talk to me."

But at first Marlene looked toward the wall, biting her lips, which had already been bitten so much they were swollen. "I'm not sure I can."

"Yes, you can."

With a small sob Marlene jerked her gaze back to Hilary. Her eyes rained tears like a bottomless storm cloud. "Oh, Hilary, promise me you won't be mad."

Just like Terri, Hilary thought, guilt clawing at her. Afraid of the unforgiving St. Hilary. How could she have failed them both so thoroughly?

"I promise," she said. "You know I love you."

"And Conner," Marlene went on, her voice rising dangerously, her fingers twining almost painfully around Hilary's. "You have to promise me you won't tell Conner."

Hilary's heart sank. Promise not to tell Conner? How could she do that?

"Marlene," she said, trying to sound calm, "I don't know if I can—"

"You *have* to!" Though her voice was not much louder than a whisper, Marlene seemed to be screaming. "I won't tell you if you don't promise. And if I can't tell somebody, I . . . I don't know *what* I'll do."

How could anyone resist such a plea? Still Hilary hesitated, some sixth sense cautioning her that if she made this promise she'd regret it.

"Please, Hilary," Marlene pressed. "I don't know what to do. Please, promise me. I need your help."

The words tore at Hilary's heart. If it was something Conner truly should know, perhaps she could talk her cousin into telling him later. In the meantime, if she refused to make the promise, who would give Marlene the guidance she seemed to need so desperately?

"All right," she said, smothering the doubt. The crisis was here, now, and she had to deal with it the best way she could. Tomorrow's crises could be handled tomorrow.

"I promise I won't tell him unless you say it's okay." She squeezed Marlene's hand. "So, what's upsetting you?"

For a minute Marlene didn't speak. She let her head fall back against the pillows, and her face was ashen under the gleaming lights. She looked so young. She *was* so young. Hilary reached out and stroked her pale brow. "Tell me, honey."

"It's about the baby." Marlene spoke with her eyes closed. "About its due date. I lied to the doctor about when my last period was, so that he'd think I wasn't due until December." She bit her lips again, and two tears seeped from under her closed lids.

"He didn't believe me, but no matter how hard he pushed I wouldn't admit anything, so he had to let it go. In front of Conner, he just says the baby's big and maturing fast."

Finally she opened her eyes, and their anguish nearly took Hilary's breath away.

"I'm really due in a couple of weeks. Maybe just after Halloween. A whole month before everybody thinks I'm due."

Hilary shook her head dully, uncomprehending. Could it really be this trivial due-date business, after all?

"Well, is that so tragic?" she asked. "Surely Conner can count. He must have already figured out that you were pregnant when you married Tommy. What's so critical about one more month?"

But even as she asked, even as Marlene's tears poured forth once more, she knew. She wasn't usually this dense, but her subconscious had been madly suppressing all hints. Suddenly the room seemed to be getting smaller, the air thicker.

One more month. But not just any month.

Marlene saw horrified recognition register on Hilary's face. "You see? Oh, God!" Her voice was high and tight, distorted by sobbing. "I hadn't even met Tommy yet!"

The room began to swirl, and Hilary closed her eyes to try to steady herself. The fatal month. The first month after Marlene had run away from home, the month nobody had ever heard much about. It had naturally been eclipsed by the ensuing news that Marlene had met and married the glamorous Tommy St. George.

"Oh, Hilary!" Marlene cried, clutching her cousin's limp, numb hand to her sodden cheek. "What am I going to do? This isn't Tommy's baby."

WHEN CONNER KNOCKED on the door twenty minutes later, Hilary and Marlene had reached a stalemate. After her tears had dried, Marlene had turned mulish, insisting that Hilary had made a solemn promise and mustn't break it. Hilary sat with her pounding head in her hands, worn out by the effort to make Marlene see that Conner *must* be told.

"But Tommy *wanted* this baby to be accepted as his," Marlene repeated stubbornly. She had reiterated that point at least two dozen times. "He knew it wasn't, but he wanted to help. He was like that, Hilary, so good and generous. I wish you'd known him—you'd have liked him. He wasn't like Conner at all."

Hilary just shook her head. She'd been through this so many times, and it seemed that nothing she said could dent her cousin's implacable determination. Apparently confession had purged Marlene's soul, and she seemed more her old self, more confident, as if she might somehow be able to pull off this nightmarish charade.

The baby's father had been a boyfriend who'd skated off into the sunset long before he'd even heard the news. Marlene had been terrified, a beauty in distress, just the kind of tragic heroine who would appeal to a young romantic like Tommy St. George.

"Conner would die before he'd help somebody in trouble," Marlene went on, still justifying her position by denigrating Conner. "He doesn't care about people. He didn't even care about Tommy, did you know that?"

Of course she knew that. Marlene had told her a hundred times. The whole conversation had been like this. Conner was so mean. So selfish. So hard-hearted. Hilary was bewildered by the girl's attitude. Did she really think that because Conner wasn't perfect, because he was, like everyone else, a flawed person, he deserved this... this ultimate lie?

Seeming to sense that Hilary wasn't about to be persuaded by her tirade, Marlene finally admitted her real reason for wanting to keep the truth a secret—her fear of Conner's wrath.

"You just can't tell him, Hilary," she moaned, tears once again close to the surface. "I couldn't stand it. You know what he'd do. He'd go crazy he'd be so furious. He'd—" shuddering, she pulled the sheet up under her chin "—he'd kill me."

"Stop saying that," Hilary said in an exhausted monotone. "You're being melodramatic and unfair." But she understood what Marlene meant. Conner would never resort to violence, but when he found out how he'd been betrayed, his anger would be... Oh, God, what a mess!

When Conner knocked on the door, Hilary's heart jumped in her chest. Suddenly she felt so poisoned by guilt she didn't think she could look him in the eye. He would hate her, too, she realized, thinking of herself for the first time. She had defended Marlene hotly from the very beginning, especially when he'd dared to hint the baby might not be Tommy's.

Marlene, how could you? She thought she'd die of shame.

But there was only one way out of the quicksand of Marlene's lie. No matter how terrible the aftermath, they *had* to tell him.

Surely Marlene could see that? In silent desperation she looked at her cousin. But the other girl just frowned, pinning her with a warning glare.

"You promised," she whispered as the door opened.

"Hi," Conner said pleasantly, obviously unaware of what a maelstrom he was entering. He pushed the door two-thirds shut behind him. "How're you feeling?"

"Terrible," Marlene responded, her voice sullen. "The doctor said I have to stay in bed for at least two days."

Conner nodded. "It's just to be on the safe side," he said. "That was Dr. Pritchard on the telephone. He's calling in a prescription for you in the morning. And he says to remind you there's nothing to worry about. He says the baby is mature enough to do beautifully even if you went into labor tonight." He smiled again. "Not that he thinks you will, but it's reassuring to know, isn't it?"

His tone was encouraging, a blatant bedside cheer, the way he might give a pep talk to a discouraged child. Watching him, it struck Hilary that she'd never seen Conner treat Marlene any other way. No matter whether she was flirtatious or petulant, he treated her like a difficult child who must be managed.

Suddenly she thought of the diamond. Surely his attitude was proof that the diamond couldn't have been bought with Marlene in mind. But what if she was wrong? What if she someday saw that exquisite ring sparkling on Marlene's finger? She rubbed her brow, trying to banish the image. No. It would never come to that.

She would *make* Marlene see that telling the truth was the only way, no matter how terrifying it seemed. She could not let this disgraceful exploitation go on. She thought it through quickly. Marlene was due in two weeks. She'd give her one week to come to her senses. One week to tell Conner the truth. And if she didn't . . .

Hilary shivered. Well, then, terror or no terror, promise or no promise, she would tell him herself.

She slept about three hours and then woke up, heart pounding, from a dream so horrible it was a mercy she couldn't recall it. She sat on the edge of the bed, coming back to consciousness slowly. And when she did, she remembered with a twisting pain that reality was worse than any nightmare.

Bunching her hair up in one fist, she rubbed the damp back of her neck with her free hand. Because Marlene had complained of a chill, Conner had thoughtfully turned up the thermostat. Now the stuffy room seemed to be closing in on her, and she longed for fresh air. Pulling her robe on over her nightgown, she opened the French doors that led to the balcony. Perhaps out here, under the tranquil night sky, she could find a little peace.

It did help. Her head felt less muddled, and she was able to think more clearly. Earlier tonight, as she'd tossed on her bed trying to escape into sleep, she had done a lot of thinking and come to some difficult conclusions. Most importantly, she had decided they couldn't wait a week to tell Conner the truth. They'd have to tell him tomorrow, as soon as Terri, who wasn't really a player in this tragedy, was safely on her plane and out of the way.

No, she corrected herself sadly, remembering that it was already three in the morning. Not tomorrow. To-day.

She thought about Connor's beautiful house, which nestled here in the forest with such a natural sense of belonging. It would be difficult to leave. She had begun to love this place.

But she would have to leave. She didn't doubt that for a minute. When he found out how he'd been duped, Conner would never again want to see Marlene or her baby or anyone to do with her.

Hilary inhaled deeply, finding the freezing air bracing. Though it would be the hardest thing she'd ever done, she would survive, and so would Marlene. Hilary's house had plenty of room for all of them—Terri, Marlene *and* the baby. And, thank heaven, her business was profitable enough that she could support everyone for a while, though not, of course, in the luxury of a St. George. Gradually, when Marlene was able to work, they would even be able to pay Conner back.

That would take a long time. In her mind's eye she saw the panoply of pretty things Marlene had acquired so greedily—hand-stitched christening gowns, brightly colored mobiles, pastel silk maternity dresses . . .

Oh, Marlene, Hilary thought with an overwhelming sense of shame. How could her cousin have found any delight in those stolen treasures?

One way or another, though, the practical part of it could be managed. They were family, and as family they would see it through together.

That much she had worked out hours ago. But here, where the air was so clear you could see for miles, she finally saw that the real tragedy in the whole mess was something she couldn't fix.

The real crime was that, when he heard the cruel truth tomorrow morning, Conner St. George would lose his brother all over again. Tommy St. George would be gone forever, and so would the baby who would have carried Tommy's memory, his genes and his bloodline into the future.

A staggering loss, one that was almost unendurable to contemplate. Hilary walked to the railing and gazed up into the moon-washed trees, wishing she could keep the sun from rising. As she watched, a few brittle leaves broke loose and sailed through the darkness into oblivion. Autumn was such a sad season. Why had she never understood that before? All this time, while she'd been admiring the fiery color and beauty, it had really been only a glorious dying.

But nature was merciful. Now that the trees were stripped nearly bare, they lifted their exposed branches to the skies. And the clement heavens responded by filling them with stars.

Those same stars sparkled and blurred as her eyes filled with tears. But she blinked them back. She mustn't cry, mustn't dwell on her own loss, mustn't think about Conner hating her. This was his tragedy, not hers.

"Tommy! Wait!"

The anguished cry rang out into the cold, empty air. Electrified, Hilary ran to the edge of the balcony just in time to hear Conner's low moan.

Now she was only a couple of feet above his door. So close. If she bent over, she could touch the glass panes of the sidelight. And against the house a small flight of steps led from her balcony to his—she could be there in seconds.

But she didn't, couldn't, move. Each of them must suffer alone. He was locked in there, in tormented sleep, and she was out here, in her own prison, too ashamed to speak, too guilty to offer tainted comfort.

But suddenly the door flew open, slamming back against the outside wall, shaking the deck. Conner burst onto the balcony, wearing only the long, loose trousers of his pajamas. Unseeing, he went right past her, as if pursued by dragons, not stopping until he reached the end of his balcony. There he spread his arms wide on the railing and dropped his head to his chest.

Stunned, she could only think how cold he must be. He was battling for air, his breath misting in quick puffs that swirled around his chest. But he seemed unaware of the temperature, unaware of everything except his internal struggle.

He had fought the nightmare valiantly, she realized, and the effort had cost him. His damp, bare skin glistened in the moonlight, and the muscles of his arms stood out like thick cords. His trousers rode low on his hips, and his hair was rumpled, falling onto his forehead in violent disarray.

Hilary squeezed her hands into fists. She longed to smooth back those black waves into a more peaceful state, to massage those straining muscles until they relaxed beneath her fingers. The small staircase that could take her to him seemed to tug at her, but she resisted. She had no right... Gradually his breathing steadied, and the perspiration dried. With obvious effort, he drew himself erect. He ran his hands through his tousled hair, turning his face toward the starry trees, just as she had only moments ago.

And then, out of the corner of his eye, he saw her. His hands froze at the back of his head, and he slowly twisted toward her, staring as if she were a ghost.

She stared, too, unable to speak. In that position, starlight splashed over the undulating muscles of his upraised arms, poured down the rippling washboard of his torso, then soaked into the soft blackness of his pajamas. It took away her breath, her voice and her soul.

"Hilary?" He lowered his arms in one fluid motion and walked back toward the house until he was right below her. "What are you doing out here?"

"I couldn't sleep," she said, marveling at the intensely masculine contours of his body. She had never realized the muscles of a man's body were so intricate, weaving in and out of one another to form a complex pattern of strength and beauty.

"Neither could I." His voice was flat, all the emotion pressed out of it as if he was trying to conceal the harrowing truth beneath the mundane statement.

And she knew that was her cue. She should have excused herself politely and withdrawn into her room until they could meet tomorrow in the civilized light of day. But she couldn't leave him, not when she knew what tomorrow held for them.

"I know," she said rashly. "You were having a bad dream. I heard you cry out."

He stiffened. "I'm sorry if I disturbed you," he said, his voice brittle. She was right—he was not a man who wanted others to witness his grief. He stepped back a pace. He could achieve a physical separation, she thought, watching him, but real distance was impossible out here. In the middle of the night, both of them half-dressed, both of them racked by dreams that would not let them rest...

How could she pretend to be a polite stranger when the very sight of him made her body ache and her nerves hum with tension as her mind replayed tormenting memories of yesterday?

"I shouldn't have put your rooms so close to mine," he said in a monotone. "I'll have Janie move your things tomorrow."

"I don't want to move," she said, abandoning any pretense of indifference. "I want to help."

At first he just stared, as if he had trouble understanding the simple words she'd spoken, but then he laughed. It was as brittle as his voice, and she heard how close he was to breaking.

"Help?" He shoved his hand into his hair again, thrusting it away from his face. "Well, that's very sweet and innocent of you, Hilary. Unfortunately there *is* no help."

His bitterness was even colder than the air around her, but she refused to let it freeze her out. He needed her. By day he might be domineering, but tonight, out here, he was vulnerable. He looked as if he hadn't slept in weeks.

"Why can't I help you?" she asked, leaning forward to bridge the distance he was trying to create. The balustrade caught her just below the breast, and her hair dangled level with his shoulders. She put out one hand. "Why won't you let me try?"

For a long minute he glared at her hand. Then he cursed and grabbed the wooden posts of the railing with angry fists.

"How do you plan to help me? Can you turn back time?" He shook the railing, like a caged animal rattling the bars of its prison. "Can you give me another chance with my brother? Can you bring back the dead?" Each word was as sharp as a fang, burying itself in her. "Because if you can't do that, Hilary, there's not a damn thing you can do for me."

But his fury didn't frighten her. She heard only his pain. Kneeling down, she wrapped her hands around his cold fingers, which still clutched the posts tightly. Her face was just inches above his now, and she met his gaze through the bars.

"No," she said, massaging his fingers softly, trying to warm them, trying to loosen their viselike grip on the wood. "I can't do any of that. But I can listen. And I can care."

"Listen to what? To a cry in the night?" His eyes were black, the starlight unable to find any of the colors that usually played there. "I wish to God you'd never heard that."

"Why?" she asked, still stroking his hands. "It's nothing to be ashamed of. You called your brother's name. That's all."

"Did I?" For a moment his anger seemed to abate. His eyebrows knitted together. "Did I really?"

"Don't you remember?"

He shook his head slowly. "No, I've never known what I say when I have the dream or even if I speak at all. I just wake up, and the room seems to be ringing with my voice."

She thought of how he had bolted through that door, running from the sound of his own screaming. "Do you ever remember the dream itself?"

With a sigh, he leaned his head against the railing, as if it was too heavy to hold up.

"Oh, God, yes," he said, shutting his eyes. "Always."

"Tell me," she said, and her hand found the dark waves of his hair. She pushed them away from his eyes. "Tell me about the dream."

"No," he whispered. Her fingers drifted down his cheek, grazing the stubble on his chin. A muscle jumped at the edge of his jaw. *"No."*

But now that her hands had found him, she couldn't seem to stop. She learned the shape of his forehead, his cheekbones, his nose, his chin, her fingers full of a wondering curiosity. His face was so unequivocally masculine—all hard bone under soft skin.

Just as she neared his lips, his eyes opened, and she saw that they were no longer black. They were full of silvery starlight.

"No," he said again, but his voice was different. It was like his face, silk-covered strength. "I don't want to talk about the dream."

Letting go of the railing, he reached through the bars and cupped her face in his hands, echoing her motions. With a pressure so light it was like a feather brushed across her skin, he traced the curve of her cheek and drew a delicate line around her mouth.

"I don't want to talk at all," he said, his voice a low growl, the satin finally thrown off to release the power beneath. He slid his hands under her hair and pulled her closer, as far as the bars would allow.

She swayed slightly and, instinctively searching for balance, wrapped her hands around the posts just as Connor had done earlier. And then he kissed her. His lips were cold, and their touch drove a bolt of iced lightning deep into her core. She shivered uncontrollably, her skin alive with a hundred thousand racing nerve endings. Her grip tightened on the posts as the kiss deepened, his mouth parting slightly, just enough for her to sense the soft, sweet warmth that lay inside.

Mindlessly she sought that warmth. She ran the tip of her tongue along the inner edge of his lower lip, and he responded with a low groan.

"Hilary," he whispered urgently against her mouth, but she couldn't answer because the kiss had claimed her breath. He probed more deeply, and she gloried in the intrusion. Boundaries melted, as the wet heat from both of them met and fused.

But it wasn't enough. The bars were in the way, denying their bodies the union that had been so tantalizingly granted to their lips. Though her eyes were shut, her mind held the vision of his body in the moonlight. A dusting of dark, crisp hairs ran in a narrow, V-shaped pattern from chest to navel, but his nipples were exposed, and they were hard, pebbling in the frosty air.

His chest would be cold, too, she thought, and she saw herself pressed against it, accepting the momentary jolt of ice so that she could find the delicious heat beneath. If only she could reach it. It was just inches from where her hands were locked around the posts. Sweep away the balustrade, and she could place her palms against those tight male nipples and warm them until they were pliant beneath her fingers. And then, when she was ready, she would make them hard again....

"I want you," she said, breathless from the kiss, which had paused only for a moment, and from her thoughts, which were even more tumultuous.

He barely took his mouth away an inch to speak. "Are you sure?"

Was she sure? Oh, yes, yes, she had never been be more sure of anything. Her breasts tingled, her nipples as tight as his. And much lower, something still latent but possessing an awesome power curled inside her. It felt like an open electrical cable, snaking slowly, sparking intermittently and ready, if touched, to set off a shock that would rock her world.

"I want you," she said again in answer, and finally he released her. She opened her eyes, and what she saw made her heart thunder in her ears. His lips were swollen, and his eyes glittered like two silver stars.

"Then come to me," he said, and he moved to the bottom of the steps, into the shadow of the house.

Shakily she rose to her feet, but looking down at him, her courage almost failed her. She couldn't see the silver fire of his eyes anymore. She opened her lips, as if to ask him something, but no words formed. If only he would come up here.

"Come to me, Hilary," he said, his voice as low and commanding as that of a hypnotist instructing his sleeping patient. And that was how she felt. Her legs were not under her own control. Her whole body seemed to belong to someone else. "Show me that you're sure."

The stairs were right beside her—just four steps and she would be in his arms. The faint voice of common sense tried to be heard over the thrumming of her heart. *What about tomorrow,* it whispered, *what about tomorrow? He's going to hate you tomorrow.*

But tomorrow didn't exist. There was only tonight, and her love for this sad and sensual man. Using the rail to guide her, she took the steps slowly, trying to remember to breathe, trying not to fall.

At the last step, as though he could wait no longer, he scooped her up and folded her against his cold, hard chest. She could feel his heart beating even through the thick velour of her robe, and she longed to cast the soft fabric aside, to feel skin upon skin, heart upon heart. Through the open French doors he carried her, then across the darkened room all the way to the other side, where the moonlight barely penetrated. When he reached the bed, he eased her slowly down, letting her body slide along his until her feet found the floor again.

She waited, breath suspended, for him to undo the clasp of her robe, but he didn't touch her. Instead, with one swift motion he untied the cord of his pajamas, and they slipped down, slithering along his muscular legs until they were just another shadow on the floor.

And then he simply stood there, allowing her eyes to grow accustomed to the dim light and allowing her to grow accustomed to his body. She could hardly believe how magnificent he was. Without speaking, she drank in every incredible inch of him. Under her scrutiny, he seemed comfortable with his nakedness, though she remained shrouded in her robe.

"Touch me," he whispered, taking her trembling hand and bringing it to his chest, to the spot where his heart pulsed just below the surface. "Feel what you do to me here." The rhythm seemed to be telegraphing some swift, urgent message, and she probed, trying to read it.

But before she could translate the code, he drew her hand slowly down the flat, muscular plane of his abdomen, and then even further, down to where a heat rose from his skin, searing her startled fingers.

"And here." Hand over hand, he showed her. "Feel what you do to me here."

She made a sound, but it was not a word. It was an inarticulate expression of wonder as her body responded instinctively to these new sensations.

"Should I be ashamed," he asked, his voice deep and thick, "to want you so much?"

She shook her head, confused by the question. Ashamed? Ashamed to be so beautiful, to be so... male?

"No," she said, reveling in what she was learning. His body was the same all over. Silk over strength, beauty over power. "Why should you be? It's..." She faltered, searching for the right word. The feel of him under her hands was distracting. "It's thrilling."

"But you were ashamed when I touched you at Fire Falls," he said. "You were ashamed of how much you wanted me."

Flushing, she met his eyes, mutely acknowledging the truth. "But that was different," she mumbled.

His eyes drifted shut, as if in memory. "You were beautiful," he said, but his voice was strained, and she felt him move against her hand. She knew what this meant, this tense, hot throbbing of his body. It meant he wanted the same wild release he had given her at the waterfall.

No, it was more than a wanting. It was a need. As the tension built under her fingers, she knew she had an ultimate power over him, and the knowledge was wildly exciting.

She knew her way now, guided by the memory of her own responses. As if realizing her growing confidence, he took his hand away. Soon, though, he groaned, and she could tell that he had reached the breaking point.

"Should I stop?" she whispered, amazed at how reluctant she was to do so. She knew he was losing control, and she loved it. An answering tension was coiling inside her own body, as if his pleasure was hers, too.

He inhaled deeply, raggedly. "For now," he said. "I think it's your turn." And finally he addressed himself to the clasp of her robe.

It yielded quickly to his sure fingers, and finding the gown underneath, he growled with a fierce impatience. But he managed those buttons, too, and he pushed both garments from her shoulders gently, exercising a superhuman restraint that she could sense even in his fingertips.

To her surprise, instead of the embarrassment she'd expected, she felt only a glorious sense of liberation, and now she knew why he had undressed himself first. Their bodies were meant for this, were clamoring for this, and at long last there was no impediment to fulfillment, not even fear.

As her clothes joined his on the floor, he let out a shuddering breath.

"You're unbelievable," he said roughly, devouring her with his eyes. "I've imagined this every day—but I could never have imagined how beautiful you are."

Then his hands joined at the feast, touching her, modeling each curve and sliding into each hollow with such expertise that within minutes she was afraid her legs wouldn't hold her any longer.

He must have known it, too. He lifted her once again, and her naked breasts were pale against his tanned chest. He took her the three short steps to the bed, and lowered her onto the mattress with a tenderness that maddened her. She didn't want him to be gentle. She wanted him to take her with an abandon that would sweep her from this mundane planet altogether.

"Make love to me, Conner," she begged, reaching for his hands. "Please. Hurry."

And as if he could read her distracted mind, he came to her with a passion beyond anything she'd ever known. His kiss was hot and claiming, taking first her lips, then her neck, then her breasts, until she was writhing under him, asking for him to touch her everywhere at once.

He read her every response perfectly. He knew what she wanted and when she wanted it. And always, the instant she was ready, he was there with more. His hands were rough without being painful. His mouth insisted, his fingers demanded. He seemed to know that she didn't want to be a fragile object he must handle with reverent care. She wanted to be consumed by this passion—a flaming, shooting star streaking across the night.

And she was, oh, she was. If only Jules could know how Conner had changed, she thought suddenly, irrelevantly. If she ever saw him again, she would tell him. Conner's hands understood everything now. He knew how to let things be what they were meant to be.

"You knew, didn't you?" Her voice was thin, her breath gasping, and she suspected her words made no sense to him. "You knew what was locked inside me, as if I were a piece of wood."

He kept kissing her, but now his path was upward, up the sensitive edges of her stomach, across her breasts, her neck, until he was poised over her.

"You're not wood, my love," he said, dropping more kisses into her hair, behind her ears, over her eyebrows. "You're definitely not wood."

"No," she answered dazedly, barely able to hang on to her train of thought. A throbbing had begun low in her abdomen, and she could feel him pressing against her, seeking entrance to the innermost parts of her. "But don't you see? You knew what I should be, even when I didn't." She must be delirious. She knew she wasn't making sense, but somehow it seemed important that he hear this. Maybe then he could stop hurting.

"No, I don't see. But it doesn't matter. Just love me, sweetheart." His shoulders were trembling from the effort required to hold back, but instead of taking pity on him, she dropped her hands to his hips, stopping him an inch away from her.

"You see, I've always thought I should be strong— but you knew better." She ignored his protest, but it was harder to ignore his hand, which crept between her legs, shamelessly trying to overcome her resistance. "You knew that I should be a star, a hot, white star—and you have made me become it."

To her surprise, he smiled. In that instant of unguarded confusion—had she said something funny?— he pressed himself into her. She gasped, losing sight of her idea entirely as the fire she had banked so briefly flamed again.

"You're wrong, Hilary," he said, driving into her, slowly at first, so slowly. His strokes were sure and hard, and both tempo and pressure increased subtly, inescapably, with every thrust. "I only know what I *want* you to be, and that's what I'm going to make you."

She shook her head, her mind imprisoned by the hypnotic rhythms, trying to catch her breath, trying to remember what she had been talking about. He was going to make her something. . . .

But it was too late. His strokes came ever faster, until she couldn't think at all. "Do you know what I'm going to make you, Hilary?"

"What?" she whispered, though she had almost forgotten the question. She had already become a star.

Did stars cry? She felt tears against her cheeks. A gloriously doomed, forever falling star. She clutched his relentlessly moving shoulders. "What are you going to..."

But she couldn't finish. Suddenly she was spinning, flying, falling, exploding into a million tiny stars, all shooting sparks of brilliant light. "Oh, Conner, yes!" she cried. "Yes!"

In an almost instantaneous combustion, her sparks, or perhaps her words, ignited his own fire. The rigid control finally broke and his rhythm grew frenzied, until it exploded in one last, shuddering burst of liquid flames.

And then they lay together, two shattered stars, dark now and lost except to each other.

"Mine," he said thickly, sleepily, and pulled her exhausted body into the cradle of his arms. "I'm going to make you mine."

CHAPTER TEN

SHE DIDN'T INTEND to sleep, determined not to lose a single second of this, her last, her only, night in paradise. She would wait, she decided, until Conner succumbed to slumber, and then she would watch over him, banishing any dragons who dared visit his dreams.

But one minute she was lying in his arms, his hand languidly stroking the dampness from her back, and the next she was listening to the angry-hornet buzz of an alarm clock and wondering what on earth it was.

Still drugged with sleep, she wriggled over to reach the night table and punched buttons at random until the hornet retreated. She shut her eyes, grateful for the silence. What a noise! Even Juliet had been awakened by the singing of a lark.

Her eyes flew open as memory flooded in. Oh, God, had tomorrow come, after all? Early-morning light gilded Conner's crisp white sheets and lay luminous, like an overflow of molten gold, on the hardwood floors. Sunlight. As different from starlight as Juliet's lark had been from a nightingale. Night's candles, as Romeo could have told her, were burned out.

But her Romeo wasn't there.

His side of the bed was already cool, retaining no imprint of his body. She slid her hands across the soft linen. He must have been gone a long time. Maybe it was *he* who had not slept.

She curled up on her side, defeated. In spite of her prayers, in spite of all that had happened in the night, tomorrow had arrived. And life as she knew it had departed.

She forced herself to look at the clock again. The inflexible numbers insisted it was seven. Had Conner set the alarm for her, she wondered? He knew that Terri's flight was at ten and that she would be waking up soon, looking for her sister. If Hilary hurried, she would just have time to sneak back to her own room and emerge, yawning and stretching like someone in a bedroom farce, with her reputation intact.

Judging by the empty sheets and the buzzing clock, that was what Conner preferred. No messy aftermath. She sat up, scanning the room, her gaze stopping on the armchair closest to the bed, which she noticed for the first time was a heavy maple four-poster. Her gown and robe, neatly folded, were waiting for her, just within arm's reach.

Automatically she glanced at the floor, where last night Conner's pajamas had pooled like liquid shadows. Nothing there, of course. How sensible. The room was pristine, all traces of their lovemaking erased, folded into precise, manageable squares or stashed away in the closet.

She snatched up her gown and flung it over her head, trying not to be bitter. When he'd said he intended to make her his, he hadn't meant anything permanent, had he? More like borrowing a book from the library, or renting a movie from the video store. Good for a couple of hours' pleasure, then back where it came from, quick and easy, with no penalties to pay.

Or maybe it was even worse. Perhaps, controlling personality that he was, he wanted to imprint himself on her fledgling sexuality, so that forevermore the act of lovemaking would conjure up the sight and feel of him, the smell of autumn in the Smokies....

Well, he'd succeeded in that. She stood up, finding herself face-to-face with a hollow-eyed woman in the cheval glass. You have no right to be upset, she told the reflection. He made no promises—not last night, not ever.

But the hollow eyes still drooped with exhaustion, with disappointment and with dread. *Don't forget,* she said to the mirror, her voice hard as glass itself, *whatever hurt he caused you is nothing compared to the pain you'll inflict on him today.*

CONNOR BREEZED into his meeting twenty minutes late, and Gil shot him a look of supreme indignation. *Three years,* the look said. *We've worked on this deal for three years, and you can't get here on time?* Conner raised his brows and smiled. *Guess not,* his own look said unrepentantly.

"Sorry, people," he said to the room at large, taking his seat. "Did I miss anything?"

His secretary placed a steaming cup of coffee at his right hand. His VP of new development slipped the architect's plans to his left. And Gil dropped the leather notebook that held the contracts in front of him with a bang.

"You know you didn't miss anything, damn it," Gil said. "We couldn't *do* anything until you got here." He tapped his watch ominously. Conner suspected Gil had been tapping his watch that way for the past twenty minutes. "The Dragon's Creek people will be here in ten minutes. Not much time for a strategy session."

"We're giving them everything they want." Conner leaned back in his chair and gazed up at his lawyer blandly. "It doesn't take a genius to negotiate a deal like that."

Gil sighed. "I'm telling you, Con, we can get them to change the clause about Phase Two. And if we take a little time here, play hard to get for one more hour, we can have a hundred grand come off the top."

"I don't want to take a little time." Conner shoved the contracts away. "I don't want Phase Two. And I don't want the hundred grand. I want to sign the damn things and go home."

"Con! A hundred gr—"

"Shut up, Gil." Conner's voice held a note of affectionate exasperation. "You're overwrought. Didn't you sleep well?"

Gil subsided into his chair. "Not as well as you did obviously," he grumbled into his coffee cup.

Conner smiled at that. He hadn't slept at all, actually, not after Hilary had come to him. Hilary. My, God, how wonderful last night had been! A rising spring of warm bubbles teased at his insides. She was the most gorgeous woman he had ever seen, and the most sensual. Her body... His hands tingled, remembering her curves, her warmth.

No, he hadn't slept, but it didn't matter. He had held her until she drifted off, and then he had simply watched her, reaching out to touch her hair, which had turned a fiery gold as dawn spilled into the room, or her arm, which lay gracefully across her breasts. It had been more restful than sleeping. He had hated to tear himself away.

Which was why he was late for this damned eight-o'clock meeting. If it had been anything but the Dragon's Creek deal, he would have canceled it. But as soon as he'd made his decision yesterday, he had kept his staff up all night finalizing the contracts. With only twenty-four hours' notice, he had forced everybody to clear their schedules for this meeting. He couldn't stand them up now. Dragon's Creek was too important.

Or so he'd thought. Now that he was here, he discovered he didn't give a damn. It was just a piece of property, not much different, really, from all the other pieces of property American Leisure Company owned. He stared at the contracts as if they were scribbles made by a greedy child, remembering with amazement that only a week ago Dragon's Creek had ruled him. It seemed like a lifetime ago. It seemed like another man, an incredibly stupid man, who hadn't yet realized that people were more important than money or deals.

Suddenly he bitterly regretted leaving Hilary for this. She shouldn't have woken up alone. They needed to talk. They needed to sort out what last night had really meant. And they needed to make love again.

But he was an hour from the house, and she was already up, getting ready to take Terri to the airport, having been awakened by the infuriating buzz of his alarm. He smiled again, liking the thought of her waking up in his bed, naked under his sheets, sated from his loving.

With effort he controlled the heat that prickled through him, for the conference-room door had opened and the Dragon's Creek entourage were filing in. He was here, and so he might as well get it over with. Conner rose and shook hands with the wary-eyed owners and frozen-faced lawyers.

What a pleasant surprise this meeting was going to be for them! Knowing his reputation, they must be expecting a prolonged dance of advance and retreat, submit and demand. But he was willing to sign, right now, right here, anything they asked him to. He'd sign his life away if it would get him home to Hilary.

And he did. Ignoring Gil's pained expression, he signed everything without a word of argument. His signature was barely legible he signed so fast.

Still, it seemed to take forever. It was nine-thirty before he signed the last contract, the one that made Dragon's Creek Resort his. He was staring at it, wondering why he felt so utterly indifferent to it, when his secretary came in.

She looked troubled, and he motioned her over.

"Mrs. St. George called," she whispered into his ear, somehow managing to convey both horror and pity. "She says it's an emergency. She says the baby's coming."

She met Conner's eyes, and her own were shining wetly. "Oh, Mr. St. George," she said, her hands clasped together. "Isn't it too soon? Too soon for the baby?"

Conner was on his feet, his heart drumming in his ears. "No," he heard himself saying. "No, it's all right. Everything is going to be just fine." Those were Hilary's words, the soothing, gentling words she had spoken yesterday. "The baby will be fine," he repeated. But when he said them, the words did not possess the same magic.

And that, he realized as he made his apologies and left instructions with his secretary, was because the magic wasn't in the words. It was in Hilary herself.

Oh, Hilary! He needed her with a physical pain. Needed her with him now. All the property in the world couldn't help him or Tommy's baby. Only Hilary, on whose strength everyone who knew her seemed to depend. Only Hilary, whose fragile body and gentle voice had finally filled the black chasm in his heart. Only Hilary could help him face whatever was coming.

And so it was then, while the dragons of fear were pursuing him out to the car, down the mountainside and all the way to the Richmond General Hospital, that he finally knew the truth.

He was in love with Hilary Fairfax.

"CONNOR, WE HAVE something to tell you. Something about Marlene's baby. It isn't your brother's child."

No, no, no. Not so baldly. He probably *would* kill them both, if she blurted it out like that.

"Conner, you know that Marlene ran away from home a whole month before she met Tommy. It was a difficult month, and she was very lonely, very frightened...."

Oh, for God's sake. Not so pathetic. He wouldn't give a tinker's damn for Marlene's loneliness once he knew the truth.

"Conner, please try to understand. Please try not to be too hard on Marlene...."

Definitely not! Too craven. He would be repelled by such groveling.

Hilary thumped the steering wheel, disgusted with herself for struggling so stupidly. There wasn't any way to sugarcoat something like this, no phrasing that could make the truth any more palatable. Marlene's situation was indefensible, and yet here Hilary was, driving home from the airport, trying to think of words to defend her.

Of course, there was the most cowardly approach of them all, the one that kept running through her mind no matter how she tried to banish it. "Conner, you have to believe me. I didn't know." Trying to save herself. As if he would believe her. As if it would make any difference, even if he did.

She drove slowly, reluctant to arrive. It was almost one o'clock. Terri's plane had been delayed, and they had eaten an early lunch at the airport while they waited, which meant Marlene would probably be querulous, feeling bored and abandoned, by the time Hilary got there. She groaned. Marlene really was spoiled. How had Conner tolerated her petulance over these past months? It made her head spin to think how glad he would be to throw them both out of his house.

Last night's frost had knocked most of the leaves from the trees, and the mountainside seemed strangely exposed. The roads all looked different without their gaudy red and yellow trimmings. Hilary, distracted by her miserable thoughts, got lost twice before she found the right road. Or maybe she was just stalling, putting off the moment she'd have to tell Marlene what she planned to do.

She knew something was wrong the minute she pulled into the driveway. The house looked empty. Soulless. Her heart skipped a beat, but she calmed herself quickly. Just a trick of the light, just a shock to see it now that the fiery autumn had been snuffed out around it.

And then she saw Janie, pacing on the lowest balcony, her arms folded tightly around her torso to keep out the chill. As Hilary drew closer, she saw that the housekeeper's face was wrinkled with anxiety.

"Miss Fairfax," Janie called, hurrying clumsily down the stairs, her arthritic knees hampering her. Hilary didn't even turn off her engine, something telling her she would not be staying. "Oh, Miss Fairfax, you need to get to the hospital." Janie was huffing, punctuating her words with short gasps. "Mrs. St.

George went into labor while you were gone. It was terrible. Her pains were only a couple of minutes apart, and she was crying."

The woman touched Hilary's arm. "Please hurry. She's been at the hospital for hours now. She wanted you there to help her."

All the blood had drained from Hilary's face, but somehow she managed to move her lips. "How did she get there?"

"She went in a taxi. There was nobody here to drive her. You were at the airport, and Mr. St. George was at his Richmond office, at least an hour away. We tried to page you at the gate. Didn't you hear it?"

Hilary shook her head. She'd heard nothing. But she hadn't been at the gate. She and Terri had returned to the terminal for lunch.

"What about Conner?" she asked numbly, almost afraid to hear the answer. "Does he know?"

Janie nodded. "Oh, yes, he's there. He met her at the hospital. But he can't help her. She's afraid of him. She wants you." She squeezed Hilary's hand and repeated, "Please hurry."

And she did. She didn't miss a single turn, driving the mountain roads as if she'd been driving them all her life. There was no time for fear, or even much caution. She kept her eyes fixed on the winding asphalt, refusing to think about what Marlene's early labor meant. She didn't want to think about how much harder it would be to tell Conner once he had actually seen the child, believing it was his own flesh and blood.

What if she was too late? What if, by the time she got there, the baby had already been born?

She stomped on the gas pedal, and her tires squealed around a tight curve. She had to get there before that happened. She couldn't let him hold the baby in his arms, press it to his chest, search its innocent face for signs of Tommy....

Worried as she was about Marlene, it was Conner's name her heart cried out. And it seemed to echo plaintively across the rolling, frost-flayed mountaintops. *Oh, Conner, Conner. What have we done to you?*

The nurse was smiling. The baby had been born an hour ago, she said. It was a girl, a tiny little girl, six pounds, but perfect. She was going to be fine. Mrs. St. George was going to be fine, too. It had been an incredibly easy labor, only four hours. Mr. St. George was in with her now.

Was Hilary a relative? Oh, Mrs. St. George's cousin? How nice! Would she like to see the baby? The nursery was just down the hall, left, then right. Hilary watched her feet walk down the corridor, first one and then the other, though she had no conscious awareness of them doing so. Left, then right. Soon now. Only a short distance away, somewhere behind a big picture window, Marlene's baby was sleeping, her delicate heart ticking away like a time bomb.

Left, then right. Until Hilary found the nursery. She was only one of several proud family members whose eager eyes searched the bassinets, hungry for their first glimpse of the infants they had waited so patiently to see.

Unlike them, Hilary brought her gaze up from her feet slowly. Cowardly though it was, she suddenly didn't want to see the baby at all, as if the birth would cease to be true if she never saw any proof of it. Oh, God, how could it be? Somewhere behind that window was a helpless bit of humanity who was going to break everyone's heart before she had even gathered the strength to lift her head.

Hilary saw Conner immediately, though his back was to her. His broad, beautiful back, which she now knew so intimately. He was clad in a somber gray business suit that exactly matched the wings of gray in his hair. Her steps faltered, and she touched the wall for balance. Conner.

He stood a little apart from the others. He wasn't looking into the nursery proper but into an adjoining room, where a few babies lay in incubators, naked under ultraviolet lights, their eyes covered with huge, circular patches.

Why? Why was he looking in there? Those babies were sick. Hadn't the nurse just said Marlene's baby was fine? Hilary parted her lips, intending to call his name, but her throat had closed, and she mouthed the word soundlessly.

Then, as if he had heard her, he turned, and suddenly she felt faint. Though she would have recognized his body anywhere, his face was that of a stranger. It was like a marble sculpture, hard, icy, lacking all human animation. And his eyes... Her knees twitched as if they might buckle. His eyes were like bits of gunmetal, and they were aimed right at her.

"Hilary." Never before had her name sounded so ugly. "Did you come to see the baby?"

She nodded, unwilling to try her voice yet. Those eyes frightened her. What was the matter with the baby? Why did Conner look so different, so cruel?

"Come, then." It was an order. "I'll show you."

She obeyed, and when she was close enough, he took her upper arm in steel fingers, thrusting her toward the window. "There she is. The second incubator."

Hilary gasped, from the pain of his fingers and from the shock of finally seeing Marlene's baby. The infant was small and pitiful under the lights, wriggling helpless limbs and mewling like a sickly kitten. She was blinded by huge patches, and her tiny hands grabbed at the empty air, reaching for something that wasn't there. Hilary thought her heart would burst.

"What's wrong with her?" she asked, her voice shaking. "Why is she here, like that?"

"Oh, it's nothing to worry about," Conner answered with false cheer. He sounded almost mad. Some grief must have driven him over the edge, she thought. And no surprise, really—it was an edge he'd been walking for months now, probably ever since his brother's death, ever since the nightmares had robbed him of sleep's healing.

"It's just a small problem," he said with that same unnatural geniality. "Just a little AB-O incompatibility. They tell me the ultraviolet lights will set everything straight."

She tried to twist around to look at him, but his hand forced her to face forward, so that she could look only at the baby. "What is an AB-O incompatibility?" she asked dully, hardly feeling the pain in her arm and hoping the rest of her would go numb, too.

"Oh, it's a simple blood problem. You see, if the mother has type-O negative blood, but the father doesn't, sometimes during delivery the baby can be exposed to blood that's incompatible with its own. It's not too dangerous, actually. Causes a little jaundice. It's very minor in this case. She won't even need the lights in a couple of days."

Hilary should have felt relieved, but she didn't. Conner's grip had not relaxed at all, and his voice was still full of something cruel, like that of a bully setting his victim up for a particularly nasty practical joke.

"Uh, then," she stammered, "what's wrong? I mean, what's wrong with..." *With you,* she wanted to say, but she didn't have the nerve. She left the sentence unfinished.

"Well," he said slowly, as if he were mulling it over in his mind. "There *is* the slight problem of the AB positive blood. Since both Marlene and Tommy are type-O negative..."

Hilary gasped, and in the glass window she saw Conner's reflection smile, a terrifying, mirthless smile.

"Ah, yes," he said. "That does need some explaining, doesn't it? Where, exactly, did we get this troublesome AB blood?"

"Conner," she began, her mouth as dry as sandpaper, her legs as weak as warm wax. "Conner, please..." She shut her eyes, trying to grab hold of her thoughts. But it was like trying to catch the water that thundered over Fire Falls. "Conner," she said, "did you talk to Marlene?"

"Yes," he said conversationally. But it was conversation with a very dangerous, seething dragon. She could hear the vicious flames beneath the pleasant tone. "As a matter of fact, I did ask Marlene about it. And do you know what she said?"

Hilary stopped breathing, stopped living. "What?"

His derisive mask fell completely away, revealing the burning fury beneath. With a ruthless jerk, he spun her around and pressed her back against the glass.

"She told me to talk to *you*."

Oh, God. His eyes were bottomless black pits, and she was about to fall into them. And she wanted to. She wanted to die right here, in his contemptuous embrace, rather than face the next few minutes.

"She said that you know all about it, and you'd be able to explain everything to me." His fingers bit into her, as if he wanted to break her bones.

"Well, I'm waiting, Hilary," he said, and it sounded like a death knell. "I'm waiting."

CHAPTER ELEVEN

EVERYONE WAS LOOKING at them. Such scenes could not be common in a place like this, Hilary thought stupidly. Conner's wrath could probably be felt by everyone within a hundred yards.

"Not here," she whispered. "Not in front of these people."

"Fine." He pulled her away from the wall and, in a mockery of chivalry, kept his hand around her upper arm, guiding her down the corridor. Neither of them spoke a word, though once or twice a sound that was halfway between a moan and a sob left her lips. Conner gave no indication that he heard anything.

They shared the elevator to the first floor with a boisterous family of five, and she was glad that the children's laughter covered their own arctic silence. When they disembarked, Conner walked with strides so long and fast she could barely keep up.

But finally he stopped—in the waiting room of the emergency ward.

Instinctively she recoiled. "Here?"

"Why not?" His eyes swept the room. "Our little melodrama will go unnoticed in this crowd, don't you think?"

Hilary looked at the crying, injured children, the white-faced wives of blue-faced heart patients, the life-weary faces of old men in wheelchairs. Yes, he was right in a way. They belonged here, among the wounded.

"Fine," she said, too tired to fight. She noticed two empty chairs in the corner—the one spot in the room from which you couldn't see the television. "How about over there?"

But when they were settled, she didn't know where to begin. She simply looked at Conner, wishing she could find, somewhere under all that anger, the man whose love she had shared last night. But that man was gone. Gone forever, exiled by Marlene's selfish lies.

"Conner," she started, swallowing hard after only one word. "I'm so sor—"

"Whose baby is it?"

His clipped words went straight to the heart of the matter, cutting across any lame excuses or drawn-out apologies she might have been considering.

"I don't know," she said, and as his face registered a cynical disbelief she hurried on. "I really don't. I never met him. Marlene said it was a brief relationship with a man she met soon after she ran away from home, but she didn't tell me his name. The man broke off the relationship before Marlene even suspected she was pregnant."

She kneaded her hands in her lap, casting only brief glances at him. "Marlene was terrified when she found out there was a baby coming. She was working as a waitress, and I'm sure she didn't make enough money to support herself, much less a child.''

He waved an irritable hand. ''Skip that part. I've seen the movie.''

She flushed and looked back down at her hands. Why did his reaction hurt her so? Hadn't she predicted he would be indifferent to Marlene's plight? Fine. She'd keep it simple and not try to appeal to his sympathy.

''Anyway, then she met Tommy. They fell in love right away, she said. When she told him about the baby, he asked her to marry him. He wanted to help.''

Conner let loose a bark of derisive laughter. ''He wanted to help?'' He repeated the words with virulent sarcasm. ''Come on, Hilary—you don't expect me to swallow that, do you? My little brother may have been naive, not to mention an easy mark for a beautiful blonde, but he wasn't a goddamn fool!''

She tried not to react, though his tone sliced through her. ''He wasn't a fool, Conner. He was a good and generous man. He wanted to raise the child as his own. He was an idealist, Marlene says, who liked to help other—''

''Marlene says?'' He started to laugh again, but it sounded more like a snarl. ''*Marlene* says? And we're supposed to take Marlene's word for it? *She'd* never tell a lie, would she?'' He ran his hand through his hair. ''Good God, listen to you! Have you accepted this heap of stinking garbage your cousin calls truth, Hilary?'' Leaning forward, he fixed his glare on her. It had the icy glint of granite. ''Or are you a liar, too?''

She stood up, knowing she had to escape. There was no point in talking to him. He didn't *care* what the truth was. His hatred and his disappointment had poisoned his mind, and he wanted only to lash out. He wanted to hurt her as he had been hurt. Well, though he may have had the right, she couldn't take it. Not today. Not from him.

"A fool or a liar? Not much to choose from between them, is there?" She held herself erect and stared at him coldly. "And what difference does it make, anyway? You've learned the truth, and Marlene's plans are thwarted. I can understand that you don't want us staying at your house, so as soon as possible we'll leave."

But even as she spoke, she realized she was hoping he would contradict her, hoping the acrimony would fall away and he would tell her to stay.

What a stupid dream that was!

Without hesitation, he nodded grimly. "I'll be out of town for two weeks. That should give Marlene time to recover her strength. When I get back, I want you both gone."

So it was over. Everything lay in ashes at her feet. She turned, trying to see the door through the stinging tears that blurred her eyes, knowing she should leave. But still she hesitated. There was something she had to tell him, though she sensed it was futile.

"I didn't know," she said, and her voice trembled like the last summer leaf in a winter wind. "I wanted to tell you that. I only found out yesterday. Last night."

Last night. She couldn't say those two words without bringing more tears to her eyes. "Last night." He raised his brows, as though surprised and curious. "Fascinating. Let's see...would that be before you came to my room, or after?"

She choked, the unshed tears tightening her throat beyond endurance. "Before," she said, the truth acid on her tongue. His face tightened, although she had thought the muscles were already as hard as any man's could be. "It was before."

"I see," he said, cocking his head to one side. "So that scene was a lie, too. But well acted. I have to say you Fairfax ladies are remarkably consistent."

Damn him! She whirled, thinking she would slap him, slap the vicious words off his cruel lips. Through hooded eyes he watched her hand rise, pull back and falter in midair—all without once trying to stop her. Almost as if he would welcome the stinging punishment.

And inexplicably her heart twisted. Never had she seen such merciless cruelty and such hopeless suffering, such hatred and such self-hatred, mixed into one tormented package. She might be a fool, but she couldn't hate him, no matter how much he despised her. She loved this lost, angry man, and she always would.

"I am sorry," she said in a broken voice, as her hand dropped to her side. "I really am so very sorry."

With a low sob she turned, praying that her legs would carry her to the door. But his voice, which sounded just like the acid she had tasted earlier, stopped her.

"One more thing, Hilary. If you should suddenly find yourself pregnant, don't bother calling me. I'm not nearly as gullible as my brother."

MARLENE AND THE BABY came home three days later—the same day Hilary discovered that Conner had nothing to worry about: she was not pregnant with his child.

She should have been happy about that, but she hadn't felt any emotion since she'd walked out of the emergency room. The fact that there was to be no baby, no lifelong reminder of that one unguarded night, simply left her more hollow, more empty, than before.

And life went on. It had to. Marlene's baby was beautiful and she flourished, in spite of her shaky beginning. They named her Laura, a name they chose out of a book, since Marlene felt no bond with her own family and had no right to use a name from the St. George family. It was all right, though. Laura suited her.

She was a good baby. Janie fussed over her, and Marlene managed quite well, all things considered. It even seemed possible, Hilary speculated with something that might have once been pleasure, that motherhood would mature Marlene as nothing else ever had.

Gil came by daily, running errands, changing diapers, making jokes, for which Hilary was grateful. She knew that by befriending them he risked displeasing Conner, but he didn't seem to care. Too bad they were going back to Florida in a few days. Given time, something might have blossomed between Gil and Marlene. . . .

Hilary shook herself. No more dreams. It was time for a double dose of reality. She and Marlene stayed up late, discussing plans for renovating Hilary's house. Which room would be the nursery? Which would be Marlene's? The young mother's spirits gradually lifted, and she seemed to begin to believe that she would survive, even without St. George money for protection. Little Laura's warm innocence helped them through the roughest spots. Finally, when Laura was ten days old, a robust seven-pound armful, they were ready to go. Leaving Marlene to finish the packing, Hilary drove into town to have the rental car filled with gas. They were driving to Florida and a breakdown on the road was the last thing they needed.

She would miss this mountain, she thought as she wound her way back up it, back to Conner's fairy-tale house in the woods. She'd miss Dragon's Creek, which twisted down the mountainside, and Fire Falls, where the dragon's power burst forth in a thundering cascade. Florida would seem very tame in comparison.

Just like her life.

For the first time in ten days she allowed pain to find its way through the layers of apathy in which she'd cocooned herself. It wasn't Dragon's Creek she would miss. It was the dragon himself. Did he still cry out in the night? She gripped the steering wheel so hard it creaked beneath her hands. And when he called out, whose soft voice would answer him?

Not hers. Never again hers. She blinked back pointless tears. *Just put him out of your mind, Hilary. You'll never see him again.*

But she was wrong. When she walked through the front door, he was there.

She froze, a grocery bag full of diapers in her arms, her mind trying to process the scene before her, though it kept rejecting what it saw, sending back the message, *It's not possible, it's not possible.*

But she knew she wasn't hallucinating. If he'd been a product of her desperate dreams, his eyes would have been full of a loving forgiveness, and he would have rushed over and scooped her up in his arms. That was what her dream had been, night after night.

This vision was very different. He stood stiffly by the empty fireplace, looking exhausted, his face drawn and hollow below his high cheekbones, his eyes merely dark shadows under furrowed brows.

And he wasn't running toward her. Quite the contrary. He wasn't even looking at her. He was looking at Marlene, who stood awkwardly behind an armchair with Laura propped against her shoulder. Marlene held one hand nervously at the back of the baby's head, as if she feared Conner might snatch the child away.

For an instant, Hilary's own protective instinct kicked in, and she wanted to shield Marlene from whatever bitter denunciations Conner had come to deliver.

But Hilary knew Marlene had earned those reproaches. It was only right that she should see what pain her lies had caused. If Hilary continued to protect her from the consequences of her actions, Marlene would never grow up. Difficult as it was, Hilary realized she had to let the two of them sort it out somehow.

With trembling legs she walked into the living room. "Hello, Conner," she said, willing her voice to betray none of her overwhelming emotions.

"Hello, Hilary." His voice was as controlled, as expressionless, as one of those computer-generated voices that greet you on corporate telephone systems. But it was still *his* voice, and she remembered how it sounded when it was thick with passion.

Her legs began to tremble. *Stop,* she commanded herself. *Stop torturing yourself.*

"We didn't expect you back so soon," she said, daring him to complain because they weren't gone yet. He'd given them two weeks. It had been only ten days, and she had been so sure they were making a safe, early getaway. "We'll be leaving just as soon as we get everything loaded in the car."

Before he could answer, she turned to her cousin. "Marlene, honey, I'm going upstairs to put these last few things in the suitcases."

"Hilary!" Marlene's cry held an accusation, as though she couldn't believe Hilary would desert her now. But Hilary ignored the tone and kept walking toward the stairs. It was time Marlene faced up to Conner and to what she had done.

She made it to her room, but once there, felt her legs give out. She fell into the chair, shopping bag forgotten in her lap, and stared out the window at the barren trees, trying to control her inner shaking.

Wasn't it hypocritical, an inner voice chided, for her to lecture Marlene about facing problems? Wasn't she running away herself? Wasn't she just hiding up here, hoping she wouldn't have to speak to him again, wouldn't have to hear him tell her what terrible things he thought of her?

Perhaps she was, she admitted wearily. But, she argued with the scolding voice, it was taking all the courage she possessed just to hold herself together, to accept what had happened and go on—and face a future without Conner in it.

She stretched her arm along the windowsill and rested her chin on it, staring out at the bare trees. The sun was weak today, and though it was after noon, rime still frosted the edges of the brook with icy crystals. The air was blue and misty, and the trees looked like complicated black spiderwebs against the sky.

The sight was depressing, though she tried to remind herself that if the trees survived the winter, they would renew themselves in the spring. Her eyes stung with needles of tears. Yes, but what a catch that was! *If* they survived the winter...

She ducked her head, resting her brow on her arm, shutting the desolate scene from view. With her eyes closed, time wandered. She didn't know how long she sat there, but it must have been long enough. Eventually she heard a car door slam, an engine come to life, a roar that gradually faded away down the mountain.

He was gone. The confrontation had been avoided. Relief and misery poured through her. He was gone.

When Marlene knocked at her door, she didn't have the energy to stand up. "Come in," she called, her voice muffled in the cradle of her arm.

The door swung open almost noiselessly. No squeaking hinges in Conner St. George's house. Only the soft brush of wood against the pale blue carpet told her Marlene had entered.

"Is he gone?" she asked, still not raising her face. Her cheeks were damp, and she needed a minute to let the tears dry. Marlene was probably looking for a strong shoulder to cry on, so she had to pull herself together.

"No, he's not."

Hilary's head snapped up and she swiveled around, her heart pumping so fast she felt dizzy. It was not Marlene who had quietly entered her room. It was Conner.

"I thought you left," she said as the room spun sickeningly around her. "I heard a car...."

He looked at her with those tired, shadowed eyes. "That was Marlene. Did you really think I would leave without talking to you?"

Of course not, she thought, squaring her shoulders instinctively. How naive she had been to think that! Lacerating Marlene wouldn't be outlet enough for his bitterness. He'd want to have a go at Hilary, too.

"All right. What did you want to say?"

Without answering, he came into the room, shutting the door behind him. He didn't look at her. He stood at the window, just a few feet from her, but gazed out into the bleak, blue air.

"Go ahead," she said angrily. "We need to get on the road soon. Say your piece, and then let me go."

Her anger didn't seem to touch him. He didn't even turn toward her.

"I wanted to tell you about my dream," he said finally, and his voice was wooden.

His dream? Her stomach lurched. He wasn't going to kill her with harsh words. He was going to illustrate the magnitude of Marlene's sin by showing Hilary the depth of his suffering. It was a diabolical punishment. Suddenly she didn't know if she could bear it.

But she had to. Though it would break her heart, she wanted to know. She wanted to understand everything she could about him, no matter how much it hurt.

"All right," she said again, clenching her hands together. "I'm listening."

After another few seconds, he took a deep breath and began.

"It's about Tommy," he said. "But of course you knew that."

She nodded, aware that he was stalling. It must be very difficult for him.

"I never really understood my brother." His voice sounded almost detached, as if he was relating a bed-time story to a child. Perhaps that was the only way he could talk about it at all. "He was so different from the rest of us, so timid and idealistic. My mother was the only one who accepted him as he was. She saw, I think, that he might have a true talent for painting. She tried to get him lessons, but my father wouldn't hear of it."

He shook his head at the memory. "I don't know why Dad was so adamant, but maybe he'd learned that attitude from his own father. My uncle hadn't been allowed to pursue his interest in art, either. For generations, everything in the St. George family had focused on business."

He laughed, but the sound died quickly. "And I was just another St. George businessman, carrying on the family tradition of stamping out all deviant behavior." He pressed his forefingers against the inner edge of his eyebrows. "God help me, I really thought I was doing the right thing."

Hilary wanted to say something, but she couldn't find any words that would help, so she kept quiet.

"When my mother was dying, Tommy was only about nine—just a kid, you know? I was twenty, so much older, so much better able to cope. She asked me to look after Tommy, to try to help him get along with my father."

He paused, and she saw a muscle twitch in his temple. "I did try. I tried to teach him to play football, to attract women, to be more aggressive, all the things the St. George family valued, the traits that would protect him from my father's disappointment—which could be pretty vicious. I made him put away his paintbrushes and take up racquetball and golf.''

Connor ran a hand through his hair. "I tried so damn hard. How was I to know it would all explode in my face someday?"

"You couldn't have," Hilary said softly. She hated to see him in such pain.

"Of course I could have. I should have." He squeezed his eyes shut. "God, it was so stupid, so backward. Tommy was miserable, and of course he made a hash of everything, which only alienated my father more."

Suddenly Hilary remembered what Jules had said about Connor's whittling a block of wood. *Maybe it would even look like a cow when he was done, but it was always a damn sorry cow, 'cause it was supposed to be a star...*

Opening his eyes, Conner gazed into the distance. "I was a fool. I hadn't understood what my mother meant at all."

Hilary dared to speak again. "What did she mean?"

"She didn't want me to *change* Tommy. She wanted me to stand up for him, to make my father learn to appreciate him. She wanted me to be his advocate." His voice thickened, clogged with self-hatred. "Instead, I became his enemy."

She shook her head, horrified. "Oh, no, I'm sure he didn't think of you that way."

"Yes, he did. Even after my father died, I kept badgering him. I made him drop his art classes and register for business management. What a mess—he failed them, of course. And he rebelled, as any kid would. He began to drink, and though I'd given him a job at the company, he refused to show up for work. He slept until noon, painted until dark and haunted the bars all night. Then he met Marlene, and he married her in spite of my opposition. Maybe because of it."

"No," Hilary interjected. He was taking too much of the blame. "He married her because he loved her."

"Maybe." Conner was following his own train of thought, and he seemed barely to hear her. "But his biggest pleasure came from defying me. If I said it was day, he insisted it was night. And like so many parents, I was too bullheaded to let it go. I had to make a world war out of every issue."

He rubbed his eyes exhaustedly. Hilary wanted to tell him to stop, to tell him he didn't have to go through it all again, but she knew that, for his own sake, he did have to. He'd kept it inside for far too long.

"And then one day he came to me, demanding the keys to the boathouse. He wanted to take out the speedboat." Connor's face was ashen in the pale light from the window. "I wouldn't give him the keys. He'd been drinking, and I didn't think he had any business driving a boat."

He placed a fist against the pane, as if he wanted to smash it but didn't have the energy. "I was so damned righteous, so determined to prevail, so sure I was protecting him. But of course he thought I was just trying to control him. He was furious, and he said all kinds of terrible things."

With a sigh he opened his fist and pressed his open palm against the glass, like a prisoner reaching for the freedom that was forbidden him. "But I still wouldn't give him the keys. I was furious, too. It had become a battle of wills."

His hand fell, and he groaned under his breath. The sound was undiluted, unendurable pain, and Hilary knew he had reached the critical point in his story.

"What I didn't know," he said, his voice almost unrecognizable, "was that Tommy had a duplicate key to the boat. He could have taken it out whenever he wanted. With all my self-righteous blustering, the only key I was actually controlling was the key to the boat-house supply room."

Hilary stood up slowly, the nightmare suddenly becoming horribly clear. "What..." The word came out as only an unintelligible rasp. She cleared her throat and tried again. "What was in the supply room?"

"Nothing, really." His voice was dead. "Nothing but some equipment. And the life jackets."

The life jackets. She stumbled toward him, her heart breaking for all the pain she *didn't* hear in his voice, pain that she knew was buried under layers of guilt and misery. Pain that was slowly killing him.

"Conner," she said, her own voice full of tears, "you couldn't have known. You couldn't have known."

"There was only one life jacket in the boat that day," he went on, the story almost telling itself. "And

Tommy gave it to Marlene. When he crashed the boat, they were both thrown clear, but his legs were broken. Without a life jacket, he never had a chance.''

Her whole head ached from trying to dam the flood of tears. She had known all this and had grieved for the doomed young man even then. But now, told in Conner's bleak, emotionless voice, the tale was utterly heartbreaking.

"Oh, my God . . .'' She took his arm, trying to hold on to him, trying to keep him from disappearing into the dark chasm of his guilt and grief.

"So, you see, every night it's the same dream,'' he went on blankly, as if he hadn't heard her, as if he couldn't feel her hands on his rigid arm. "I run after him, down the dock, holding out the keys, begging him to take them. But the dock just keeps getting longer and longer, and I can never reach him. He's always just ahead of me, and he doesn't hear me calling.''

He turned to her, his eyes unfocused, as if he couldn't see her through the haze of pain. "That's why I wanted the baby to be his. I wanted another chance, you see. A chance to make it right. I was crazy, I think, when it came to that baby. I even sometimes hoped I might be able to talk Marlene into letting me raise it, at least some of the time. When I was in Florida, I drove over to see a woman I'd been dating—I even had a diamond ring with me—and was going to ask her to marry me—to help me create the kind of home Tommy's baby would be happy in.''

The ring! The beautiful, sparkling diamond that Hilary had found tossed in a kitchen drawer. So it hadn't been intended for Marlene. There had been some other woman, someone Hilary had never heard of. She tried not to think how close she must have come that night to losing him. "Who was she?" Her mouth felt like dust. "Were you in love with her?"

"No, I wasn't, not even a little—that's how insane I was. But I couldn't do it. I got all the way to her house and then I couldn't get out of the car. I think some part of me realized how crazy it was." He leaned his head back. "But I was desperate, Hilary. I—"

"I know," she said, putting her hands on his chest, as if that action could still the hammering of his heart. "Oh, Conner, I do understand."

He grabbed her arms. "Do you? Can you?"

She nodded, and his grip tightened. "I wanted to kill someone the day I found out about the baby," he said. "Marlene or you. Or myself. I was insane with it."

"I know," she said again. She put her hand up to his face. The skin was rough, imperfectly shaved, and drawn so tautly it felt like stone. "It's all right, Conner. It doesn't matter."

"Yes, it does." He leaned into her hand, as if it were a cradle. "I don't see how you can ever forgive me."

"I already have," she murmured, hardly knowing what she was saying, hardly aware of what his words meant. She was only aware that he was suffering, and she had to help him. "It's over."

"I've arranged a settlement for Marlene," he said, shutting his eyes and letting her hands roam his face as he spoke. "And a trust for the baby." He named a figure so high it made her heart skip a beat. "She should have plenty to live on for the rest of her life, just as Tommy would have wanted."

Hilary's hands froze. Had she heard him correctly? "But—" her words were tangled up in knots "—why did you do that? If you really think Marlene tricked him into marrying her..."

"I don't think that, Hilary," he said, and he sounded utterly defeated. "I'm not sure I ever did."

Hilary caught her breath on a sob she couldn't suppress, and Conner put a finger against her lips.

"I've done a lot of thinking these past few days," he said. "And I finally see what I have to do. Tommy's gone. I can't have another chance to show him that I loved him just the way he was. All I can do is honor his memory, honor the values of tolerance and generosity that he represented, by carrying out his wishes. I can give Marlene and her child the security he wanted them to have."

Tears were coursing down Hilary's cheeks, and she parted her lips, unable to breathe. "Conner," she said, her voice breaking, "you don't have to do that. She was wrong, so wrong...."

"I've been too hard on her," he said quietly. "It's because I've never really been able to forgive her for being alive while Tommy is dead. Maybe that was why I couldn't see how much love his decision to give her the only life jacket reflected. I couldn't even see how truly noble that was."

He looked deeply into Hilary's eyes, searching for something he seemed to need, something he seemed to fear he wouldn't find. "Even in his drunken fury he was determined to protect the woman he loved. He would rather die than let anything happen to her."

With trembling fingers he touched the tears that scored her cheeks. "Maybe I understand it better now because, for the first time in my life, I feel that way about someone, too. I would do all those things and more for you."

She didn't dare believe what she'd heard. "For me?" she whispered, and her eyes held a breathless question.

"For you, Hilary." His voice was husky. "Only you. And perhaps," he said, brushing the tears away with gentle thumbs, "perhaps, someday, for our child. I can't help hoping there will be a child, Hilary, that maybe the night you came to my room we created a new life...."

She shook her head, tears coming so fast now he couldn't sweep them away. They ran around his fingers like a swift stream around a fallen branch, an uncheckable, salty current of emotion.

"No," she said, remembering the hollow feeling, the emptiness. "No, we didn't."

With a ghost of a smile, he kissed the wetness under each eye. "Then we'll have to try again." He kissed her soggy cheek. "And again and again, until we do."

She could hardly speak. A geyser of happiness had suddenly erupted inside her, drowning rational thought and coherent speech. "Do you mean that you... that we..."

"I mean I can't live without you," he said fiercely, his hands tightening as if he thought she'd pull away. "I mean if you leave here today I'll come after you, and somehow, some way, I will make you mine."

His. Oh, if he only knew!

"You already have," she said. "I've been yours since the first day you touched me, and I'll be yours until the day I die."

His eyes searched her face, their depths at first full of a simple determination to possess her, then, as they read her soul, softening into a look of such tenderness that their gaze was almost a caress. She was still crying, but these were tears of joy that seemed to cleanse her as they fell.

"And I'm yours," he said gently. "It's the only thing I'm sure of anymore. Everything that mattered to me before I met you seems pointless now. When I bought back Dragon's Creek Resort, it was supposed to be the happiest day of my life. But it didn't mean a thing. I lost you that day, and I thought I'd die. If only I could have you back, I thought, I'd gladly give up all of it."

Although the intensity of his emotion moved her beyond measure, she tried to smile. The result was merely a tremulous parting of her lips. "Oh, no," she managed to say. "You have to own the dragon!"

"Why?" He frowned lightly, his thumbs moving over her face, across her trembling lips. "I don't need it. I don't need anything but you."

She leaned into his touch. "Yes, you do," she insisted, sighing against his hand. "I want you to take me back to Fire Falls. I want to be able to put No Trespassing signs everywhere, so all that beauty will be ours, and no one can disturb us. It will be," she said, kissing the outer edge of his hand, "our own special heaven."

At the touch of her lips, a fire leapt into his eyes. It flashed, like an arcing current, from his gaze straight into the very core of her. And its heat burned her tears away in one searing instant. There would, she somehow knew, be no more tears. . . .

"Heaven," he repeated. Slowly he bent his head toward her. "Do you want me to take you there now, my love?"

She nodded, her body alive with desire. She wanted it more than she wanted the air she breathed.

Scooping her into his arms, he carried her to the bed and lay her across it. She waited, her heart fluttering against her breast, as he discarded his clothing. She marveled at how steady his hands were. Her own felt numb and helpless, incapable of loosening even one of her buttons.

But he was capable enough for both of them. Kneeling over her, he began to open her blouse, kissing each satiny patch of skin as he exposed it.

Finally, when their clothes were no longer between them, her hands found their purpose and their strength, rising up the muscular length of his thighs, over the bones of his hips, and around to the hollow of his lower back. She pressed him closer, guiding his desire home to hers.

Someday, in the future that surely would be theirs, there would be time for patience, for a slow loving. But now their need swept all tamer emotions aside. He took her, driving into her with a storm of longing, a gale of passion.

With the desperation that only two people who had given up hope can feel, they clung to each other as the storm built and swirled, then finally broke in a tidal wave of sensation that obliterated everything in its path.

Afterward, she lay weakly in his arms, her head against his chest, his chin against her hair.

"I love you," she said, and her voice was barely audible. "I love you so much it hurts."

She sensed his languid smile. "No, my love," he said drowsily, pulling her closer. "Nothing hurts in heaven."

And then, for hours, while the afternoon slipped away into a golden sunset, a silver twilight and finally a dreamless night, Conner St. George slept.

HARLEQUIN®

PRESENTS® *plus*

Meet Helen Palmer. She knows that as *single* mother of the bride, she's going to have to spend time with Zack Neilson, *single* father of the groom. Trouble is, Zack's the man responsible for her broken heart.

And then there's Charlie MacEnnaly. When it rains it pours! Not only is she forced to accept the hospitality of business tycoon Phil Atmor—her only neighbor on Norman's Island—she's forced to bunk in with Sam, Phil's pet pig.

Helen and Charlie are just two of the passionate women you'll discover each month in Harlequin Presents Plus. And if you think they're passionate, wait until you meet Zack and Phil!

Watch for
MOTHER OF THE BRIDE by Carole Mortimer
Harlequin Presents Plus #1607

and

SUMMER STORMS by Emma Goldrick
Harlequin Presents Plus #1608

Harlequin Presents Plus
The best has just gotten better!

Available in December wherever
Harlequin Books are sold.

When the only time you have for yourself is...

STOLEN *moments* ™

Christmas is such a busy time—with shopping, decorating, writing cards, trimming trees, wrapping gifts....

When you do have a few *stolen moments* to call your own, treat yourself to a brand-new *short* novel. Relax with one of our Stocking Stuffers— or with all six!

Each STOLEN MOMENTS title is a complete and original contemporary romance that's the perfect length for the busy woman of the nineties! Especially at Christmas...

And they make perfect **stocking stuffers**, too! (For your mother, grandmother, daughters, friends, co-workers, neighbors, aunts, cousins—all the other women in your life!)

Look for the STOLEN MOMENTS display in December

STOCKING STUFFERS:

HIS MISTRESS Carrie Alexander
DANIEL'S DECEPTION Marie DeWitt
SNOW ANGEL Isolde Evans
THE FAMILY MAN Danielle Kelly
THE LONE WOLF Ellen Rogers
MONTANA CHRISTMAS Lynn Russell

HSM2

 **WØRLDWIDE LIBRARY**

POSTCARDS FROM EUROPE

HARLEQUIN PRESENTS®

Hi!
Spending a year in Europe. You won't believe how great the men are! Will be visiting Greece, Italy, France and more.
Wish you were here—how about joining us in January?

There's a handsome Greek just waiting to meet you.

THE ALPHA MAN
by Kay Thorpe

Harlequin Presents #1619

Available in January
wherever Harlequin books are sold.

HPPFEG

Harlequin is proud to present our best authors and their best books. Always the best for your reading pleasure!

Throughout 1993, Harlequin will bring you exciting books by some of the top names in contemporary romance!

In November, look for

BARBARA DELINSKY

First, Best and Only

Their passion burned even stronger....

CEO Marni Lange didn't have time for nonsense like photographs. The promotion department, however, insisted she was the perfect cover model for the launch of their new career-woman magazine. She couldn't argue with her own department. She should have.

The photographer was a man she'd prayed never to see again. Brian Webster had been her first— and best—lover. This time, could she play with fire without being burned?

Don't miss FIRST, BEST AND ONLY by Barbara Delinsky... wherever Harlequin books are sold.

1993 Keepsake

CHRISTMAS

Stories

Capture the spirit and romance of Christmas with KEEPSAKE CHRISTMAS STORIES, a collection of three stories by favorite historical authors. The perfect Christmas gift!

Don't miss these heartwarming stories, available in November wherever Harlequin books are sold:

ONCE UPON A CHRISTMAS by Curtiss Ann Matlock
A FAIRYTALE SEASON by Marianne Willman
TIDINGS OF JOY by Victoria Pade

ADD A TOUCH OF ROMANCE TO YOUR HOLIDAY SEASON WITH KEEPSAKE CHRISTMAS STORIES!

HX93

**Fifty red-blooded, white-hot, true-blue hunks
from every State in the Union!**

Look for MEN MADE IN AMERICA! Written by some of our most poplar authors, these stories feature fifty of the strongest, sexiest men, each from a different state in the union!

Two titles available every other month at your favorite retail outlet.

In November, look for:

STRAIGHT FROM THE HEART by Barbara Delinsky (Connecticut)
AUTHOR'S CHOICE by Elizabeth August (Delaware)

In January, look for:

DREAM COME TRUE by Ann Major (Florida)
WAY OF THE WILLOW by Linda Shaw (Georgia)

You won't be able to resist MEN MADE IN AMERICA!